MYSTERIES IN OUR NATIONAL PARKS

MYSTERY

MYSTERIES
IN OUR NATIONAL PARKS

Deadly Waters

GLORIA SKURZYNSKI AND ALANE FERGUSON

SCHOLASTIC INC.

New York Toronto London Auckland Sydney
Mexico City New Delhi Hong Kong Buenos Aires

ISBN 0-439-53758-4

12 11 10 9 8 7 6 5 4 3 2 1   3 4 5 6 7 8/0

Printed in the U.S.A.   40

First Scholastic printing, March 2003

Map by Carl Mehler, Director of Maps;
Thomas L. Gray, Map Research;
Michelle H. Picard, Martin S. Walz, Map Production

Acknowledgments

The authors are sincerely grateful to
the experts who have helped with this book.
Captain David S. Nolan of the real *Pescedillo;* Teri
Rowles, Fishery Biologist of the National Marine
Fishery Service; Sentiel Rommel, Research Scientist at
the Florida Department of Environmental Protection's
Marine Mammal Pathobiology Laboratory;
Tom Pitchford, Assistant Research Scientist at the
Florida Department of Environmental Protection's
Marine Mammal Pathobiology Laboratory; John
Tyminski, Shark Biologist at the Center for Shark
Research, Mote Marine Laboratory; Captain Frank and
Georgia Garrett of Majestic Everglades Excursions;
The Everglades City Sheriff's Office Substation.
In Everglades National Park, our sincere thanks to
Jim Brown, Maureen McGee-Ballinger,
and Rangers Kelly Bulyis and Carl Hilts.
A very special thanks to
Skip Snow.

To Danny and Kathy,
who radiate grace and bring us joy.

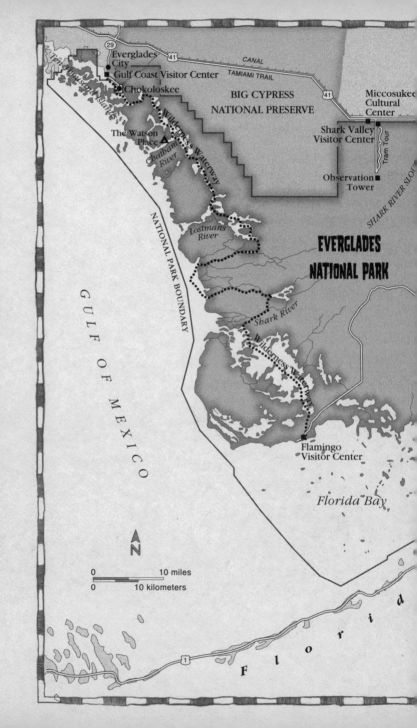

FLORIDA

EVERGLADES
NATIONAL PARK

Miami

TAMIAMI TRAIL

*Biscayne
Bay*

Homestead

Florida City

st F. Coe
tor Center

■ Point of interest
▲ Camping site

ATLANTIC

OCEAN

PARK DATA

STATE: Florida

ESTABLISHED: 1947

AREA: 1,506,539 acres

CLIMATE: Subtropical. Rainfall averages 60 inches each year. From mid-December to mid-April it is usually warm and dry; from mid-April to mid-December it is hot and humid, with lots of mosquitoes.

NATURAL FEATURES: Freshwater sawgrass marshes, pinelands, mangrove forests and islands, dense stands of tropical hardwood trees, extensive estuaries and open-water marine habitat.

The snake's five-foot body stretched across a thick tree limb overhanging the Everglades waters. Its unblinking black eyes watched the man. For a brief instant, the man's gaze locked onto the snake's before he returned his attention to the object in his hands. "Good thing a snake doesn't talk," he told himself. "I'd have to kill it." Mosquitoes whined around him, landing on his arms, but he didn't bother to swat them off.

"Whatever it takes," he told himself. "Almost done." There was no room for mistakes, not on something like this. He had to be careful, careful....

And then he saw them, three figures huddled on the wooden dock, two boys and a girl. They were far away, a couple hundred yards, maybe, but they were staring in his direction. And one of them was pointing something. A camera!

The snake flicked its tongue before it slowly wound

its way down the tree to disappear into the dark tangle of mangrove roots. Coolly, the man started up the engine of his boat and headed it toward the dock, toward those kids.

"Whatever it takes," he told himself again.

CHAPTER ONE

Upstream, two round alligator eyes blinked just above water. The gator was middle-size: about five feet from its tail tip to its blunt nose. As it skimmed forward, it left behind a rippled wake that barely disturbed the canal's surface. While Jack Landon fumbled for his camera, his sister, Ashley, pointed, following the path of the dark shape in the water. The gator was closing in fast.

"Look, Bridger, he's after that duck, or whatever it is," Ashley murmured to the boy standing beside her. "Should I yell to warn it?"

"Gator's got to eat, too," was all Bridger answered. A tall, lean, tow-headed 14-year-old wearing a Stetson hat, jeans, and cowboy boots, Bridger Conley had already proved himself to be a boy of few words. And strong opinions.

The three of them—Jack, Ashley, and Bridger—stood beside a canal in the Florida Everglades, watching the large bird that kept swimming underwater, with its whole body submerged. Every minute or so the bird's small head and long, skinny neck would snake upward, breaking through the sun's reflection on the water. Then back down it would go, gliding beneath the surface like a seal. It didn't seem to notice the danger it was in.

"Hold it...hold it," Jack muttered, twisting his lens to focus. Catching both animals in one picture would make a magnificent shot. Jack knew the bird didn't have much of a chance, not with those quick jaws and razor-sharp teeth coming nearer and nearer as the alligator quietly shortened the distance between them.

"I don't think I want to watch this...," Ashley began, her hands clutching the wooden railing.

Seeming unconcerned, the bird ducked its head beneath the water and came up with a small fish speared on its beak. Immediately the bird's rope-thin neck snapped like a whip. Momentum flipped the fish into the air before it fell back into the open beak. As the bird swallowed its catch, the alligator slid even closer, advancing through the grass-edged water, only inches from its prey. Closer, and....

With a splash, the alligator struck—too late! One split second before the big jaws snapped closed, the bird had exploded skyward, leaving the gator with nothing but a mouthful of air. If an alligator could look disappointed, this one did.

"Yes! My duck made it! It got away!" Ashley pumped

her fist into the air as she gave a little half-bounce. "Did you see that, Jack?"

"Yes, I saw it," he answered. "Only it isn't a duck, it's an anhinga."

"How'd you know that?" Bridger asked.

"Read about it in the visitor center. Anhingas swim submerged. Look at it now, on top of that tree—it's drying its feathers." Silhouetted against the sky, the bird seemed to be posing for Jack's camera, stretching out its wings to warm itself in the sun.

"Well, whatever it's called, I'm glad the gator didn't get it," Ashley said. "I know you said everything in the food chain's got to eat, Bridger, but I hate seeing an animal get killed. I don't even like to see fish die, but I guess that kind of thing doesn't bother *you,* since you said you like to go fishing."

"Doesn't bother me at all," Bridger answered.

He was the latest in a series of foster children who'd lived short term with the Landon family: Jack, Ashley, and their parents, Steven and Olivia. Bridger was unlike any of the other foster children the Landons had sheltered. He seemed friendly enough; he just didn't talk much. For Ashley, who talked all the time, this made Bridger a real challenge.

"Still, don't you feel sorry for fish when they flop all over, trying to get back in the water?" Ashley persisted.

"Nope. They're just fish," Bridger said evenly. "People are people, critters are critters."

Jack slapped a mosquito off his arm. "Better not let Mom hear you say that. She's brought us all the way to Florida to try and save the manatees, which I guess to you are just 'critters.'"

When Bridger shrugged, Jack felt prickles of irritation. Everyone in his family, from his father to ten-year-old Ashley, loved animals, but Bridger seemed almost indifferent. How could anybody not care about the manatees? "You know, Bridger, all the park rangers are freaking out over the manatees getting sick. This is serious. They're an endangered species."

"Yeah, Mom was up all night, reading through stuff and trying to figure out what could be wrong," Ashley added. "She says none of the other marine life in the Everglades is getting sick, but some of the manatees have started to die. Not all of them, though. Mom told me it's the most mysterious case she's ever been called on."

Jack took a sip of bottled water and scanned the sky for another possible photo shot. Normally he wouldn't try to keep a conversation going with a guy like Bridger, but since his dad encouraged him to reach out to the foster kids, Jack searched his mind for something else to say. That was one of the harder things about foster kids: Jack couldn't just walk away from them without seeming rude. It was like they were guests in the Landon house. "Well, anyway, you might hook something major tomorrow, Bridger, when we go fishing. Dad says Frankie's the best guide around here. And the Everglades has freshwater fish and saltwater fish. Lots of big ones."

When Bridger nodded in reply, Jack recapped the bottle, then leaned over the wooden railing to get a better look at the water below.

A hundred feet away, downstream, stood the round building that housed the Shark Valley ranger office, where Jack's mother and father were gathering as much information as they could about the temperature, rain cycles, and wildlife of the area. Here in Shark Valley, and in all the rest of Everglades National Park, lived birds and animals and marine life that Jack had never seen before. Strange, exotic breeds that, if photographed just right, could maybe make a picture good enough to get published in a magazine. Jack had saved his money for almost a year to buy a telephoto lens he'd dreamed of owning ever since he could remember, a lens powerful enough to bring distant objects into crystal-clear view.

"Bridger, did you know that Frankie's taking us kids all the way toward the Gulf of Mexico tomorrow?" Ashley chattered. "Mom's here to concentrate on the manatees, so Frankie's going to keep us busy. Except I've decided I'm not going to fish, I'm just going to sit in the end of Frankie's boat and watch for manatees."

Jack was startled by a loud smack as Bridger smashed a mosquito on his neck. "Buggy here," he said. He pushed his Stetson back on his head, then wiped the sweat from his pale eyebrows. All the Landons were in T-shirts, shorts, and sandals, but Bridger had insisted on wearing his usual Western clothes, in spite of the Florida heat and humidity. Squinting against the bright sun, he asked Jack, "So, are you gonna stick your pole in the water? Or are you afraid of hurting some fish's feelings, like your sister is. Not that there's anything wrong with that. It's just...girls." He smiled, shaking his head.

"Hey—what do you mean—'just *girls?*'" Ashley stuttered, her cheeks suddenly bright.

Bridger shrugged. "No offense. Most females feel like you, worrying about animals same as if they were human. Guys are different. We're natural-born hunters. Right, Jack?"

"Don't ask me. I fish, but I don't hunt. The only thing I shoot is pictures." Snapping the lens cover back onto his camera, Jack tried to give his sister a look that would tell her not to let Bridger's comments get under her skin. They already knew that Bridger had a different way of looking at things.

The first night Bridger had come into the Landons' home he'd told Steven how great it was that he was a wildlife veterinarian.

"No, it's not me, Bridger," Steven had corrected him. "My wife, Olivia, is the veterinarian. I'm a photographer—well, when I'm not running the photo lab. My favorite job is to follow Olivia around, photographing the animals she's working with."

A look of confusion had spread across Bridger's face.

"You mean you work for your wife?" He'd said it as though it were the strangest thing he'd ever heard.

"Not really," Olivia had answered. "Oh, I couldn't do my job without Steven's help, but he doesn't *work* for me. See, Bridger, whenever an animal or certain species is in trouble, the National Park Service calls on me to investigate. Steven comes along to take photographs. Lots of times I miss things that I discover later when I examine Steven's photos."

Olivia seemed ready to say more about married people helping each other, but she caught herself. Before Bridger came to their home, a social worker had told the Landons about his background—that his parents were divorced and his mother lived far away in Australia, that she'd left him when Bridger was only five years old. "Tell us about your dad," Olivia had said instead.

"My dad's a bull rider. You've heard of him, right?" Bridger had looked from Olivia to Steven expectantly. "Skip Conley—the Rodeo King?"

Olivia shook her head no, explaining that even though the Landons lived in Jackson Hole, Wyoming, in the heart of cowboy country, she'd never really seen a rodeo. "If I had, I'm sure I'd have heard of your father," she apologized.

"He's a star. Twelve-time finalist, eight-time bull-riding champ. Soon as he's out of the hospital, me and him'll be back on the rodeo circuit."

"We heard your dad got gored by a bull, but he'll

be OK," Steven said, his voice assuring.

Olivia nodded. "And we're glad to have you stay here with us, Bridger, until your dad gets well."

"Thanks, ma'am. Dad got slammed pretty bad on his last ride in Jackson Hole. Rest of the rodeo's moved on, but Dad's gonna be in that rehab place for a while longer. After he gets out, we'll go back to the bulls and broncs on the circuit." He could understand it, he'd told Olivia, that she didn't know about his dad, her being a woman and all.

That's when Jack had figured out that Bridger viewed the world differently, with girls on one side, guys on the other. And now, after being in Florida for less than a day, he'd announced to Jack that guys were hunters and girls weren't, as if everything and everyone fit neatly into life's spaces.

"Look!" Ashley exclaimed. "The alligator's coming back again."

The gator's snout had broken through the upside-down tree reflections, making the branches ripple on the water's surface. Once again the big jaws opened and snapped, and this time the gator caught his dinner—a red-bellied turtle.

"I can't watch!" Ashley cried as the powerful jaws crunched right through the turtle's shell. "It's horrible!"

"Gator's got to eat," Bridger said again. "Right, Jack?"

Jack was so intent on capturing the scene that he didn't answer. He fired off shots as if his camera were a machine gun spitting bullets. The pictures wouldn't be pretty, but they'd be powerful.

With a final crushing bite, the gator flung back its neck and gulped down its prey, then slowly lowered itself into the murky water.

"Right, Jack?" Bridger asked again.

"Let's go find Mom and Dad," was all Jack answered.

CHAPTER TWO

Spray me, Mom."

Ashley stretched out both arms as her mother took aim with the can of bug repellent. "Mosquitoes sure do love you, honey," Olivia said, covering Ashley's arms with a fine mist. "Turn around so I can get the backs of your legs. Maybe you should have worn jeans, like Bridger, instead of those shorts."

"Jeans are too hot," Ashley answered. "Anyway, it's not fair. I get all chewed up, and Jack hardly has any mosquito bites at all."

Their father, Steven, said, "It's because you're so sweet, Ashley."

She started to giggle. "That must mean you're sour, Jack."

"Hey, I can handle personal rejection from mosquitoes," Jack answered. "No problem! But I'll put a few squirts of that stuff on me, too, just in case." The bite of insect repellent filled his nose as Jack squirted his skin. "Here you go, Bridger," he said, ready to toss the canister, except that Bridger held up his hands like a traffic cop.

"Don't need it," he said, which was probably true. Bridger was so covered up by his long-sleeved plaid shirt, blue jeans, boots, and Western hat that any mosquito would have had a hard time finding a place to land on him.

Olivia raised her eyebrows. "You sure about that, Bridger? Try guessing how many different species of mosquitoes live in the Everglades."

"Don't know," Bridger said.

"Twenty!" Ashley guessed.

"Nope. Forty-three. But only the females bite."

Bridger asked, "So why don't they get rid of the mosquitoes? You know, spray stuff from airplanes and kill them all?"

"Can't do it," Steven answered, scratching his wrist where an early-breakfasting mosquito had already sampled him. "Much as we don't like mosquitoes, they're part of the ecosystem."

Bridger frowned. "Eco—what?"

"That means," Olivia began, "that all the creatures in the Everglades are linked together. Mosquitoes lay eggs that hatch into something called wrigglers, and they get eaten by *Gambusia*. That's the scientific name, but usually they're called mosquitofish. Other fish eat the mosquitofish: snook, snapper, redfish—the ones you'll be fishing for today, Bridger. And then, of course, birds eat the fish, and other animals eat the birds, all the way up to the biggest animals in the park. If you take out the mosquitoes, everything gets affected."

"I get it," Bridger said, nodding. "Chain reaction."

"No spraying for bugs, huh?" Jack considered that. "So then it can't be pesticides that are making the manatees sick."

"Actually, the park people checked out another possibility, Jack, that herbicides used to kill weeds in the canals might have washed into the Everglades waters. But when they did the necropsies on the dead manatees—"

"What're 'necropsies,' Mom?" Ashley interrupted.

"A necropsy is an autopsy on an animal. Anyway, the necropsies didn't show any high level of herbicides in the manatees' tissues. So it's something else," she told them, frowning. "And the biggest part of the puzzle is why only about 20 percent of the manatees are getting sick. The rest seem just fine. That's the reason they brought me here: to find out what's happening with these sick sea cows."

"Cows?" Bridger asked, his pale brows knitting together.

"Not your kind of cows," Steven answered, laughing. "Sea cow is just another name for manatee, and not a very accurate name. Manatees are distant relatives of—get this!—of *elephants*." Olivia put the half-empty can of bug spray into Jack's camera bag as she added, "They call them cows because they graze on plants all day, just like dairy cows."

"OK, everybody," Steven called out, "time to get into the car. Frankie will be waiting at the dock."

As the three kids jammed side by side in the car's backseat, Ashley explained to Bridger, "Frankie was my grandmother's friend even before my mom was born."

"Hmmm," Bridger murmured, peering out the car window. Not too far from them, the waters of the bay sparkled in the sunlight. As Steven maneuvered the car along a palm-lined two-lane road, past houses that looked like boxes with legs, Bridger asked, "How come all these houses are built up on stilts like that?"

"Hurricanes?" Jack suggested, and his father agreed, "Uh-huh. When hurricanes cause big waves to surge up over the land, houses built high on pilings don't get damaged as much."

"Looks like they could just get up and walk away," Bridger murmured.

"Yeah, they do look like that. That's a good one, Bridger," Steven told him, grinning as they pulled over in front of a general store near the water.

Ashley shouted, "There's Frankie, waiting for us."

Scanning the sidewalk in front of the store, Bridger started to say, "I don't see—" But by then Ashley had darted out of the car and into the arms of a short, wiry, white-haired woman.

"You've grown so big!" the woman was telling Ashley, as Olivia, Jack, and Steven caught up with them. "And Jack—look at you! Twelve years old and you're almost as tall as a man."

"Frankie, it's great to see you again!" all the Landons exclaimed as they hugged her.

Half in disbelief, then in alarm, Bridger exclaimed, "Frankie is a woman?"

Taking his hand, Olivia pulled him forward and said, "Bridger, I'd like you to meet Captain Frankie Gardell, the best fishing guide in all of the Everglades."

With his eyes narrowed to a squint, Bridger touched the brim of his cowboy hat and mumbled, "Pleased to meet you, ma'am." At first he looked anything but pleased, but then his face lightened a bit as he said, "Guess you just *own* the boat, right? Who runs it for you?"

"Me!" When Frankie smiled, the skin around her mouth crinkled into dozens of wrinkles that connected to other dozens of wrinkles in her sun-browned cheeks. She was small, barely over five feet two, and dressed in a red-and-white-striped shirt that hung over cutoff jeans. It seemed odd, even to Jack, for a 70-year-old woman to wear cutoffs, but somehow on Frankie it looked all right.

"To answer your question, Bridger," Frankie went on, "when my husband, Gene, was alive, we made the fishing trips together. But Gene's been gone for eight years now, rest his soul, and in that time I've run this business by myself."

Bridger looked even more confused. "Your husband's name was Jean?"

Chuckling, Frankie answered, "Spelled G-E-N-E. Short for Eugene. And I'm Frankie, short for Francesca. And yonder's the *Pescadillo*."

Thoroughly flustered, Bridger burst out, "What the heck is a pescadillo?"

"It's my boat! The name is kind of a combination of *'pesce,'* which is Italian for 'fish,' and 'peccadillo,' which means—well, I'll tell you later, Bridger. We need to get moving."

"Good idea," Olivia said, glancing at her watch. "I have a meeting in 20 minutes. Lots of people coming: park rangers, researchers—everyone with information on the manatees. I feel as if I've got a thousand pieces of a big puzzle, Frankie, and no picture on the box to guide me. So do you mind if Steven and I leave now and don't see you off?"

"Go, go!" Frankie urged them, shooing Steven and Olivia with sun-browned hands. "My new shipmates and I will be just fine. Won't we, Ashley?"

"You bet!"

Steven said, "Then we'll see you tonight. Get busy out there, guys—if you make a good catch, the restaurant will cook it for us."

From the end of the dock, the four of them waved, watching Steven and Olivia pull away in the car. Once they'd disappeared, Frankie placed her hands on her hips and surveyed the kids. Jack wondered if she could tell that Bridger was unhappy about her being a woman, but if she knew, she didn't let on. Instead, she began to bark out orders like a real ship's captain.

Pointing briskly, she went down the line. "Jack, you load up the rest of the gear that's right by your feet. Bridger, you take that cooler on board and stow it between the captain's chair and the gunwale. Ashley, you're going to get the line off the piling, and when I tell you, throw it onto the boat deck and then jump in after it. Don't wait too long, or the boat'll get away from you and you'll end up with an Everglades bath."

"I'll untie the boat for her," Bridger offered.

"Nonsense. Ashley's as agile as a monkey. You handle the cooler, and Ashley will take care of the rest. But first, Bridger, take off those boots!"

For a moment, Bridger stood stock still, his face reddening slightly to match the red in his plaid cotton shirt. "Why?" he asked.

"No boots on board! They'll gouge the deck. If you don't have any boat shoes with you, like Jack and Ashley are wearing, then you can just stay in your sock feet."

Bridger got even redder. Finally, touching the brim of his hat, he said, "Yes, ma'am," so softly that Jack was sure Frankie hadn't heard, except that she sent another smile in Bridger's direction. He sat down to take off his boots.

Jack jumped down into the *Pescadillo*. From there

he reached up to the dock to pick up the gear, one box at a time, transferring it into the boat. Bridger, still on the dock, lifted the cooler and set the boots on top of it, intending to hold everything while he lowered himself into the boat.

"Maybe you ought to...," Jack began as Bridger put one foot on the boat's edge, which Frankie had called the gunwale. But Bridger shook his head. He wobbled a little—the cooler was heavy, the boat moved from the dock under the pressure of his foot, and his socks must have felt pretty slippery on the teakwood gunwale. Jack halfway reached out to help, but Bridger frowned in concentration, as though this were some kind of athletic competition, and by sheer willpower he could figure out how to balance himself and his heavy load on the narrow rim. And he did. After sizing it all up, he took one more step and then jumped, landing flatfooted in the boat, with his balance and the cooler intact. He didn't grin in satisfaction, but just gave a short, sharp nod to no one in particular, stowed the cooler beside the captain's chair, and set his boots alongside a white vinyl bench.

Out of the corner of her eye, Frankie had watched the whole episode. All she said was, "Hop to it, Ashley. All aboard that's goin' aboard." Ashley undid the line from the cleat on the piling, threw it into the boat, then scrambled quickly after it.

"All right, crew, line up and get your life jackets,"

Frankie ordered. "One per customer—pull them out of the box there."

"What about you, Frankie?" Ashley asked. "You need to wear one too, don't you?"

"Um...ah...," Frankie hedged, and then said, "Yes, you're absolutely right. Watch me and you can see how to buckle these things." After they'd all slipped their arms through the pillowy orange life jackets and fastened the straps, Frankie said, "Now let's shove off and see what we can find out there in the land of Ten Thousand Islands." In an instant the diesel engine caught and roared. Jack could feel the vibrations under his feet.

"Sticking close to shore the way we are now, I've got to go slow," Frankie told them. "The water's no more than four feet deep here, which makes it easy to run over manatees, something we definitely don't want to do."

Even their slow passage stirred up a nice breeze, enough to whip Frankie's hair into short white spikes that looked like peaks of meringue. Surely, deftly, she handled the steering wheel as though she and the boat were lifelong friends. After a while, Frankie told them, "The trick to maneuvering through these mangrove islands is to know where the channels are. We've passed the town of Chokoloskee now, so I'll let her out a little." She pushed the throttle forward on the starboard side of the helm.

"We were in Chokoloskee last night—" Jack had started to say, but before he could get it out, the

Pescadillo leaped forward and his words were sucked back into his throat.

"Wow! This is *great!*" Ashley cried loudly, so she could be heard above the motor and the sudden rush of wind. "Feels like someone just turned on the air conditioning." She stood at the helm, next to Frankie, who effortlessly steered through the tea-colored water.

Cupping his hands around his mouth, Jack called, "How fast can this boat go?"

"Seventeen knots when we're in the Gulf." The boat's bow pushed toward turquoise sky as Jack and Bridger settled back onto the white vinyl bench. Bridger kept reaching up to hold onto his hat, until a gust of wind almost whipped it off his head into the boat's wake. Grudgingly, he pushed his Stetson underneath the bench. Jack noticed a white band of skin that stretched from Bridger's eyebrows into his pale hair, as though his forehead had never seen sunlight.

Jerking his chin toward the front of the boat, Bridger said, "That Frankie's kinda bossy, isn't she?"

"Maybe. But I like her," Jack answered.

It seemed Bridger was about to say more, but he stopped when Ashley turned, wide eyed, to yell, "Jack, Bridger—look over the right side of the boat!"

"Starboard," Frankie corrected. "Seems like we've got ourselves an escort. There's another one portside, too."

Jack leaned over the side as far as he could reach. Water sprayed his face in a cool mist, and the teakwood gunwale felt wet beneath his fingers. He had to strain forward until he saw them. Next to the boat's bow, leaping into the air like silver streaks of light, were two dolphins. For once, Jack didn't reach for his camera. He didn't want to pull his eyes away for even a second; magically, the dolphins disappeared into the water, only to reappear like the flash of needles through satin. "They love the waves the boat makes," Frankie called over her shoulder. "They're playing with us."

Over and over again, the dolphins shot up through the bow waves, turned on their sides, and slapped the white, foaming water. Once, when Bridger leaned out too far, one of the dolphins clapped its tail hard enough to splash him in an amber shower.

"Hey—*watch it!*" he shouted.

"They're rascals," Frankie laughed. "Don't feel bad, Bridger, they've gotten me many a time, too. Dolphins are some of the smartest animals on this planet. Sometimes I think they've got us humans beat."

Scowling, Bridger bent down to lift his Stetson from beneath his seat. Water dripped off its rim in a tiny rivulet. "Dang!" he muttered. "Soaked. My socks, too."

"Say good-bye to the dolphins, kiddos. We've got to slow down again, and they'll only play with us if there's a wake to jump in." When Frankie pulled back on the throttle, the waves died to a ripple. As if on cue, the dolphins glided away and disappeared from sight.

Only then did Jack realize that he'd let them get away without taking a single picture.

Even though the boat rocked beneath her, Frankie seemed rooted to the deck floor. With one arm outstretched, she pointed to a narrow passage that sliced between two islands of mangrove trees.

"Down that way—see where I'm pointing? Some of the best fishing in the Everglades is in there. If you're not afraid, I'll take you to fish near a special spot called the Watson Place."

"What do you mean, 'afraid?'" Bridger asked. He shook his Stetson, trying to get the wet drops off the hat.

Frankie's eyes, clear and blue, glinted like jewels against leather. "Before I take you all the way down to the Watson Place, I need to know if you kids have heard any of the—stories—about what happened there. I myself pay them no mind, but if any of you is skittish, we can head to another fishing area."

"If it's got the best fishing, then let's go," Bridger announced. "Jack, are you with me?"

The answer was easy for Jack, since he'd never even heard of the Watson Place, but when he looked at Ashley, he could tell she knew something. Her eyes had widened, and she bit her lower lip. "I—don't know," she stammered.

"Ahh, you've heard about Watson's landing, have you?" Frankie gave Ashley a knowing smile, then patted her shoulder. "Well, now, don't go believing everything you hear, although I myself have seen some strange things happen around that island."

Bridger shook his head and muttered, "Girls! Now we'll miss the best fishing." He aimed the comment at Jack as though he didn't want Ashley to overhear. Then, louder, Bridger said to Frankie, "OK, ma'am, you take us wherever you think's best."

But Frankie wasn't listening. She peered ahead intently, somewhere off the starboard bow. Slowing the boat to a crawl, she shaded her eyes with her hand to get a better look.

"Over there...," she began, pointing.

"What?" Ashley leaned forward, shadowing Frankie, trying to see. Jack, too, jumped to his feet, staring over the glassy surface.

"In the direction of the Watson Place. I'll try to get closer. I can't tell what it is for sure, but there's something strange floating in the water."

CHAPTER THREE

Jack thought his own vision was sharp, but Frankie had noticed the mound floating in the water long before any of the three kids could make it out. She maneuvered the boat closer, and closer, until....

"It's a pelican," she announced, her voice tight with worry. "All tangled up in a fishing line someone dropped into the water. I get so angry when this happens—that line's going to kill it!"

When Jack and Ashley hung over the side of the boat to get a look, the big bird frantically tried to flap out of the way. Its bright yellow eyes watched them like a beacon light. Only one of its wings could move at all; the other wing was held awkwardly against its body by the nearly invisible fishing cord. "We can cut it loose, can't we?" Jack asked. "Then it'll be OK."

"If we can get it without hurting it. That'll be harder to do than you might think."

No one had been paying much attention to Bridger, who was standing behind them. "How deep is the water right here?" he asked.

"No more than six feet," Frankie answered.

Jack turned to see Bridger pulling off his left sock; the right one already lay on the boat's deck. Before Jack realized what he was going to do, Bridger eased himself over the side, so there wouldn't be a loud splash.

"Good boy, Bridger," Frankie said. "He can't peck at you—his bill is tied tight against his neck. Just watch out for the loose wing so you don't break it. That's the way—come around behind him. I'll get my big net."

Bridger's orange life jacket floated up from his chest, held by the straps. The drenching had plastered his blond hair against his forehead. He shook his head to get the drops out of his eyes, then quietly treaded water, slowly coming closer to the panic-stricken bird. His lips were moving; he seemed to be talking to it. Then, with a big splash, he threw his arms around the pelican's body.

"Gently, gently," Frankie cautioned. Holding the net by its long handle, she slipped it into the water. "Try to get him in headfirst," she told Bridger. "That's it. Good! Jack, as I raise the net, you reach over and grab the frame. Great! That's the way. Ashley, you give Bridger a hand."

Ashley clung to the gunwale as Bridger took her hand and half leaped to haul himself into the boat, grabbing the gunwale with his free hand. Rivulets of tea-colored water dripped from his shirt and his jeans.

"We won't take the pelican out of the net," Frankie was saying, "or we might hurt it more. Look, there's an even worse problem—that fishhook's torn a big hole in its throat pouch. Oh! That's bad, really bad. If that wound isn't treated with antibiotics, the pelican will get an infection and die. It's happened before."

"Poor thing's scared to death," Bridger muttered "Look at its eyes." The round, glassy eyes rolled in their sockets as the bird struggled futilely to free itself.

Fingers flying, Bridger unbuttoned his long-sleeved plaid shirt. Beneath it was a white T-shirt, dripping wet like the rest of his clothes. Without saying anything, he wrapped his plaid shirt around the pelican's head, right over the net. For a long moment he held his hands steady on the bird's body. That seemed to calm it.

"Gotta think what to do," Frankie murmured. "I should get this bird to the animal rescue people right away, but I don't want to spoil our day...."

For a moment Frankie stayed silent as Jack and Ashley exchanged looks. Then, looking up suddenly, Frankie asked, "Bridger, how old are you?"

"Fifteen in three more months."

Frankie studied Bridger, who was struggling to pull off his wet T-shirt so he could wring it out. "I think you're a boy who takes a hard look before he leaps," she said. "But you also react fast in emergencies. That's good. So here's what I'm considering. I'll take you kids over to the Watson Place—"

Ashley gave a sharp little gasp. No one except Jack noticed it.

"It's not too far from here. There's a picnic table where you can spread out the lunch I brought, and then you can fish from the dock while I take this pelican back to Everglades City. If I go like blazes, I can get there and be back in an hour and 40 minutes, two hours at the outside. While I'm gone, Bridger will be in charge."

Jack felt a pang of resentment. "Why Bridger? Anyway, Ashley and I don't need a baby-sitter, Frankie."

"I'm the skipper here," Frankie declared, her voice stern, "and I say Bridger's the first mate while I'm gone. Got it?"

Reluctantly, Jack nodded, resisting the urge to say "aye, aye" and salute.

"Now, Bridger," Frankie went on, "I'm going to move the boat fast, so I think it'll be good if you hold your hands on the pelican like you did before, to calm it as much as possible. The engine noise is going to scare it something awful."

As the boat picked up speed, Frankie shouted to be heard over the sound. "Couple of rules, here, kids. Stay in the clearing around the Watson Place. Don't—repeat, *don't*—go into the mangrove forest. These mangrove forests grow so dense that even folks who are used to these parts get lost in 'em."

Frankie took one hand off the steering wheel to wave at the masses of trees growing on each side of the waterway passage, forests so impenetrable they looked like the tufts of a plush green carpet. Above the waterline, tangles of roots wove together like wicker cages, reaching down into water turned brown by tannic acid from the trees.

"One more reason to stay out of the mangroves—that's where the mosquitoes are really bad. They can suck you dry."

Frankie stayed silent for a moment, slowing the boat so that it was easier to hear her. "Bridger, I said I'd tell you what 'peccadillo' means. It means 'foolish mistake.' Gene and I sometimes wondered if we were foolish to work here where mistakes can be deadly. Tropical storms, snakebites, mosquitoes that swarm so thickly after dark they can suffocate you—out here, if you guess wrong, bad things happen. But in spite of the risks, we decided it was worth it. This is where we wanted to be."

Bridger nodded. "I understand, ma'am. My dad would understand, too."

"So I'm trusting you," she went on, "to make good decisions. Now look, over there on the right, up ahead. That's the Watson Place."

They'd been moving fast enough that the breeze, plus the heat, had nearly dried Bridger's T-shirt. His arms were already starting to turn red from the sun, but again he refused the sunscreen Ashley offered him. Why did Frankie think Bridger was so responsible, Jack wondered, when he did dumb things such as letting himself fry?

They eased the boat next to a rickety dock made of weathered planks; the dock stretched into a walkway that butted against a narrow shore of silty mud. Beyond that, Jack saw a clearing, filled with grass and ringed in a thicket of mangrove trees. Two picnic tables hunkered near the shoreline. Near them, on a pole, was a brown sign that said "Watson Place," and beneath that, a warning: "No Campfires," with a red circle and a line through it. The sign reflected upside down in the glassy water.

"OK, Jack, hop out and pull 'er close to the dock. Bridger, you'll need that cooler in case you get hungry or thirsty while I'm gone. Ashley, you start unloading the fishing gear. I'm going to try and secure this pelican."

The four didn't talk as they busied themselves with their jobs. Frankie managed to knot one of the shirt sleeves to the pedestal at the base of the pilot's chair, which kept the pelican tethered. On the dock, the gear was lined up in a neat row alongside the stacked-up life jackets; the green cooler sat next to them. Jack's muscles strained to keep the boat wedged against the dock until Frankie gave the signal for him to throw in the line. A moment later, as the *Pescadillo* accelerated, Frankie turned and cupped her hands to shout, "I'll be back in an hour and 40 or so. *Stay put.*"

"We will, Captain," Bridger called back.

The three of them waved until the boat disappeared

around a mangrove bend. Then Ashley glanced nervously over her shoulder, her lips pressed into a tight line.

Bridger smoothed the rim of his cowboy hat before pushing it firmly on his head. He'd already pulled on his socks and boots, and except for the missing plaid shirt, he looked exactly as he'd looked earlier. "I want to scout around the Watson Place before I start to fish," he announced. "Want to come, Jack?"

"Sure."

"Hey, wait, I'm not staying here on this dock by myself," Ashley protested.

Bridger rolled back on the heels of his boots. "I figured you wouldn't want to check the island out, seeing as how jumpy you are."

"That's because...you don't know...."

"Don't know what?" Bridger pressed.

"Nothing," Ashley muttered, setting her jaw in a way that meant she wasn't going to talk anymore. From experience, Jack knew that if something was bothering her it would come out sooner or later. It was best to let Ashley settle things in her own mind. Whatever it was, she'd reveal it soon enough.

After they stepped off the dock and onto the shore, they headed for the ring of trees huddled around the edge of the clearing. Some of the trees were different from the ever-present mangroves, and Jack guessed someone must have planted other varieties to break up the monotony of the mangroves' black, gnarled limbs and webbed roots. Or maybe these were exotic trees, as he'd heard them called, that didn't belong there, that had washed in from the Gulf and threatened to take over the native trees.

As they walked, tall grass brushed against Jack's bare shins like thousands of fingers. He tried not to let himself think that snakes might be crawling in the dense underbrush. Bridger didn't seem bothered by the thought of bugs or reptiles; maybe it was because his boots would protect him from almost anything that could bite at an ankle.

The cleared space was cut in the shape of a half-circle whose edges touched the water. Jack saw grass crushed into flat circles and rectangle shapes. Campers must have stayed here. Even though the sign said "No Campfires," charred tree limbs and a couple of burned spots told him someone had disobeyed the warning.

It didn't take them long to explore the open field. "What's that thing over there?" Jack asked. "Looks like a big pot with a bunch of bricks around it."

"It's for making syrup," Ashley answered.

Before Jack could ask her how she knew such a thing, Bridger broke in with, "There's some concrete over there that a house must have stood on once, but nothin's left."

"Probably blew away in a hurricane," Jack said.

They ended up back at the picnic table where their cooler now sat. Jack flipped open the latch and pulled out some colas, handing one to Bridger and one to Ashley.

Pushing back his hat, Bridger surveyed the landing and said, "Watson, whoever he was, must have cleared this spot. Would have been hard. I've cut my share of sagebrush at our place in Montana. Land always wants to go wild again."

"This used to be an ancient oyster-shell mound," Ashley said quietly. "From the Calusa Indians. Bloody Watson took it over and turned it into a farm in the 1890s. Behind that big poinciana tree is another 40 acres where he grew sugar cane and did...other stuff."

Surprised, Jack asked, "'Bloody Watson'? When did you learn about this place?"

"Yesterday, when Mom took me to Smallwood's Store in Chokoloskee to buy postcards. That's when the lady in Smallwood's told me all about it."

"All about what?"

"The things that went on out here, at the Watson Place." Biting her lip, she added, "I don't think you want to hear about it. We can't leave this place, at least not for a while."

Bridger snorted. "Ghost stories? Girls are always believing stuff like that." He winked at Ashley in a way Jack knew Ashley would hate and added, "I'm not afraid."

"They're *not* ghost stories, Bridger," Ashley shot back. "Everything I heard about is true. A Calusa medicine man warned that a lot of bad things would happen unless people listened to him and changed their ways. No one did. And the medicine man was right. The Watson Place was cursed!"

One corner of Bridger's mouth lifted slightly in a lopsided grin.

"I'd like to hear the story," Jack told his sister. "Tell us what happened. Why'd they call him Bloody Watson? And what did the Indian medicine man say?"

Ashley pulled back the can's flip top and let the hiss escape into the muggy Florida air. "You're sure you want me to tell?"

"Positive."

"OK. Just don't blame me if you want out of here when you hear the story."

CHAPTER FOUR

More than a thousand years ago, the Calusa Indians lived in the Everglades. They used oyster shells to build mounds, and over the centuries the mounds rose high above water to make islands. Soil piled up on these islands, turning them into rich farmlands where the Calusas lived in harmony with animals and nature.

After the Civil War, white men discovered this place. By the 1890s, many hunters came here to kill birds for their feathers and alligators for their hides. In those days, egret plumes were used to decorate ladies' hats; the white, fluffy feathers were actually worth more than their weight in gold. So many egrets were killed that they almost died out. And tens of thousands of alligators got slaughtered. But the hunters skinned only the alligators' undersides— that was the most valuable part of the hide—and left the rest to rot in the hot Florida sun.

"The earth is bleeding," the Indians said, and it really

was. "If this killing doesn't stop," a medicine man warned, "the land will be cursed. More blood will spill— the blood of men who don't respect all Earth's creatures."

It was just about then that the mysterious man called Bloody Watson arrived in the Everglades. With his family, he came right here, to this very spot we're standing on, to this mangrove island that started out as a shell mound built by the Calusa Indians so long ago.

"I'm not interested in hunting critters," Mr. Watson told everyone. "All I want to do is farm and grow sugarcane." Mostly he was very polite, tipping his hat and saying "Howdy" to the folks at Chokoloskee and Everglades City. He paid his bills on time at the grocery store and made the best sugarcane syrup in southern Florida.

Mr. Watson always wore a black hat and a black frock coat, and beneath that coat he carried a gun, a .38 revolver. He could whip out that revolver faster than a man could blink, and he had a deadly aim.

Everglades City was a wild town, back then. Desperadoes showed up, stayed for a while, and vanished back into the fog and the mangrove forests. Some were never seen again—at least not alive. Whenever a man got killed, Mr. Watson usually was blamed for it, even though he might have been miles away.

Folks around these parts spread stories about Bloody Watson, trading rumors at night behind windows shuttered tightly against mosquitoes. They whispered that he was a cold-blooded killer.

Each time Mr. Watson walked into a store or tavern, the other men acted real nervous. Mr. Watson kind of enjoyed that. If he could scare people, he figured, he could do pretty much anything he wanted to in the Everglades. When anyone dared to question him, he'd stare at them with his steely blue eyes, give a little smile, and say, "You know I never killed anybody—except in self-defense."

The same folks never worried much about the Indian curse. "That's just Injun superstition," they'd say. "They only tell it to keep us from huntin' on their land."

One day a couple of fishermen were rowing close to here when they saw something sticking up in the water. Something large and gleaming white, like the underbelly of a fish. Except—it had toes! It turned out to be a human foot.

They pulled out two bodies, one a woman who'd been Mr. Watson's cook, the other a man who'd tended hogs on the Watson Place. When people came to investigate, they found a third murder victim—a foreman on the plantation. And in the barn, swinging from a rope, was the body of a young Indian woman. She'd hanged herself!

Mr. Watson said he'd been away on his boat when the murders took place, but he got accused anyway. By then, the townspeople of Chokoloskee decided they'd had just about enough of Bloody Watson. They blamed him for all the bad things that were happening around here, and they began to plot against him.

Twenty men, all armed with shotguns and rifles, gathered on the shore in front of the store owned by the Smallwood family, just waiting for Mr. Watson to arrive in his boat.

"If we all shoot him at once," they reckoned, "why, then, they can't blame any one of us fellers for his murder." When Mr. Watson arrived by boat and stepped onto the shore, all 20 men shot him at the same time. They kept on firing even after he fell dead, pumping 33 or more bullets into him, not counting buckshot. His blood reddened the ground.

They buried Mr. Watson on a lonesome sand bar not far from here. But the troubles weren't over. For many years the slaughter of the animals continued, and the Indian curse hung over this land like a shadow. When another family moved into the Watson house, here on the island, they found bloodstains on the walls. No matter how hard they scrubbed, the blood would never wash off....

Bridger scoffed, "What'd I tell you? A ghost story! A place is just a place, Ashley. These trees—just trees. Grass—just grass. No bodies in the water. No curse."

"I'm not scared of bodies," she said. "It's just—maybe other bad things could happen while we're here! Maybe the old Indian curse is still working. How do we know it isn't?"

Turning to Jack, Bridger raised his eyebrows. This time he didn't say "Girls!" but that's what the look meant. Instead, he swatted at the mosquitoes on his arms and asked Jack, "You think Frankie might have some of that bug juice in the box of fishing tackle? These mosquitoes must think I'm a T-bone steak, the way they're chewin' on me."

"I have some in my camera bag." Jack found the can, and this time Bridger squirted it all over himself. Jack and Ashley sprayed themselves again, too, because the mosquitoes were thick, and the repellent did seem to keep them from biting.

After that, Bridger pulled out the fishing gear and the portable canvas seats Frankie had given them. Ashley moved up and down the boardwalk, rubbing her arms as if she were cold, which Jack knew was impossible in the 90-degree heat. Maybe she was just trying to rub the repellent farther into her skin.

With a sure, quick motion, Bridger baited his hook, then silently handed Jack the plastic tub of minnows. Ashley was suddenly at Jack's side, her dark eyes big and round.

"Wait—Jack—you're not going to stick a hook through that little minnow, are you? It's still alive!"

"Live bait's the best kind," Bridger answered her. "Mr. Watson used live bait, too, I bet—'cept maybe it was people, not minnows." He laughed out loud.

"Ooooh! That's sick!"

"Lighten up, Ashley, I'm just kidding you. You can't let stuff like that story get to you."

Ashley narrowed her eyes at Bridger. "I guess you're not scared of anything 'cause you're a guy, right?"

He scratched the skin under his ear. "Well...," he said slowly, "me and Jack just heard the story, and we didn't freak out. Guys are different, I guess. Watch your brother now—he's gonna bait that hook, no problem. Right, Jack?"

"Right." Actually, Jack wasn't too comfortable about putting a hook through a live minnow; before, when he'd gone trout fishing in Wyoming, he'd always used artificial flies. His parents had taught him that every living creature, no matter how small, was valuable and had a right to life. And Ashley's story about the slaughter of the helpless animals still hung in his mind.

But then, he'd been slapping mosquitoes all day, and they were living creatures, weren't they? Thrusting his hand into the tub, he brought up a wriggling minnow.

"Jack, don't!" Ashley cried.

But he did.

Bridger smiled approvingly. "See? Nothin' to it. You can look now, Ashley. Jack threw his line into the water."

When Ashley uncovered her eyes, they looked mad. "Just because I don't want to see a little fish speared doesn't mean I'm not as tough as you guys," she snapped. "Besides, why should I have to kill a minnow to catch a big fish so I can kill that, too, and eat it? Would that prove I was brave or something? How do you think the fish feels?"

Expertly casting his line overhanded, Bridger said, "Didn't see you turn up your nose at that Big Mac you ate yesterday. Where do you think hamburgers come from, a hamburger tree?"

Ashley colored. "That's different."

"Not to the cow, it's not," Bridger told her, laughing at his own joke. "You know, I hope you're right about the Indian curse on this place, Ashley. I'm hoping bad things happen to a couple of big snappers. You hear that, fish?" Cupping his hand around his mouth, Bridger called into the water, "You're under the evil spell of the Watson Place. Bite my hook."

That was more words than Jack had heard Bridger say all at once since he'd come to stay with the Landons. He was actually making jokes that were even kind of funny, Jack had to admit. Rolling her eyes, Ashley went to the end of the dock and flopped down, cross-legged, her back to them.

Jack watched Bridger's red-and-white bobber gently float in the still water, like a round, sightless eye.

"You better cast farther out," Bridger advised him.

"Yeah. It's just, the water's so dark, you can't see what's down there."

"What difference does that make? You think there's a skeleton in the water?"

"Sure. Right." Jack reeled in, checked his bait, raised his arm over his head, and tried to cast the way he'd seen Bridger do it. Jack had only been fishing two or three times, and he was far from expert. As his line landed—15 feet closer to the shore than Bridger's—the two boys settled into the quiet rhythm of fishing.

The steady hum of insects throbbed in the hot air, like a human heart beating from inside the shadowy trees. Could there be a body, one no one had found, hidden among the mangroves just yards away from where he sat? Stupid, Jack scolded himself. Stop thinking about stuff that happened nearly a hundred years ago. If there'd ever been a body over there, it would have been long gone by now.

Indian curses—things like that weren't even real. Still, he couldn't shake the feeling that something bad was about to happen. The mangrove roots seemed to claw at the Everglades like gnarled fingers; he thought of that cook's foot sticking up out of the water. Whew! He needed to get his mind on something else. Bridger's right, Jack decided. Guys need to be tough.

Ashley didn't help. "Jack, I keep seeing circles coming up in the water over there." She pointed in the opposite direction from where the boys' lines were creating their own ripples.

"Circles?"

"Yeah. Little, round water wiggles that keep rising to the surface. It's like...like someone's trying to breathe underwater."

"Oh, come on, Ashley!"

"But I saw them! Over there!"

"If you want to think up weird things with your imagination, keep it to yourself," Jack grumbled, but he did glance over once or twice to where she'd pointed. He didn't see any circles in the water.

Overhead, an osprey skimmed the treetops, then dove to the water's surface and scooped up a large silver fish that writhed in its talons. Suddenly another, larger bird swooped in at close range, dive-bombing the osprey.

"Look at that!" Ashley cried, pointing to the birds.

Squinting at the sky, Bridger asked, "What? A ghost?"

"It's a bald eagle!" Jack answered. "Man, I can't believe we're this close to it. I think the eagle's trying to steal the osprey's fish. Look at the wingspan on the eagle—it must be six feet! I've got to get my camera! Ashley, can you hold my pole?"

"OK. Hurry, Jack. That'll be a great shot!"

It was all over before he could even get the lens cap off. The eagle won. Its fierce stare and curved beak must have spooked the osprey into giving up its dinner; the eagle flew up to a tree branch to enjoy its stolen meal. It's a rough world out there in the mangrove swamp, Jack decided. Big fish eat little fish, and hostile birds steal from weaker ones.

Peering through his telephoto lens, he followed along the edge of the mangrove forest, examining the weird shapes of the roots. A certain clump of them looked awfully solid for roots, he thought. He twisted the lens to get whatever it was into focus, and realized he was looking at a big bull alligator sunning himself on the bank.

Just stay where you are, big guy, Jack told it without saying so out loud. Don't come down here where we are. But even as he thought that, the alligator slowly slid into the water. In a moment Jack knew why. The gator had been scared away by the faint sound of a motor coming around the bend, to the south of the Watson Place.

A boat moved into the camera's viewfinder. And it wasn't Frankie's boat.

CHAPTER FIVE

Even through the telephoto lens, Jack couldn't get a good look at whoever was piloting the boat, since the craft was still too far away. From the person's height, he guessed it was a man. Using the most powerful setting he had on his zoom lens, he watched the man halt his bullet-shaped boat beside some pilings that stuck up out of the water like matchsticks. When the man finally cut the motor, the Watson Place was quiet once more, except for the ever-present buzz of insects and the sound of water lapping against the dock.

"Hey, look up there, the birds are fighting again," Ashley exclaimed.

Jack's attention was caught by the osprey, still trying to find dinner. It scooped up another fish, and once more the eagle came after it. This time Jack was ready. He kept firing off one camera shot after another, not sure if he got anything, because the birds moved as fast as shooting stars. This time the osprey won the battle. With its sharp beak, it tore the fish to pieces and swallowed it, triumphant.

"All right, osprey! There's justice," Bridger said, shading his eyes as he peered into the sky. "What's the other bird to the right of it?"

"A great blue heron," Jack answered excitedly. "I can't believe we get to see so much different wildlife on this trip. The Everglades has everything!" The heron flew gracefully overhead, silhouetted against the sky, close to where the man had stopped his boat. When the bird settled on a mangrove root, Jack finished off the roll of film, taking half a dozen pictures of the heron.

"Hey, Jack, if you're gonna fish, then do it," Ashley complained. "If you keep taking pictures, I'm putting down the pole."

"OK, I'm coming. Hold on just another minute." Quickly he changed film and dropped the used roll inside one of the gear boxes. Carefully he set his camera on the splintery wooden dock, then thought better of it and put it inside the gear box with the film.

While he was fussing with the camera, he heard the engine fire up again; the boat in the distance had left the pilings and was chugging toward the Watson Place.

"Look, he's coming our way," Bridger commented. "He'll probably go right by us."

"I don't think so," Ashley said. "He's coming right for us. I don't think we should talk to strangers."

"Ashley, for heck's sake," Jack answered crossly, "if he stops here at this dock, what are we supposed to do—ignore him? He's just some fisherman."

As the boat came closer, Jack admired the man's piloting skills. He was able to maneuver around Bridger's fishing line without snagging it, and he pulled up exactly at the end of the dock, cutting the motor to a slow idle. The boat bobbed in the wake, but the man moved with the boat as easily as Frankie had, as though he'd been born on the water.

"Hi, kids," he said pleasantly. "When I saw you three all alone out here, I thought I'd check things out and make sure you're OK. Is everything all right?" The man was tall and thin, wearing an expensive-looking short-sleeved shirt that stopped just above his elbows, revealing bronzed skin the color of a penny. The blond hairs on his arms had been sun bleached until they gave off an almost metallic sheen in the light, which seemed at odds with his coffee-brown beard. He wore knee-length khaki shorts that were surprisingly crisp, since most everything else was wilting in the Everglades humidity, including Jack. He couldn't help but think this person looked a lot more put together than Frankie.

"What makes you think we're alone?" Bridger asked, sounding wary.

"Well, there's no boat docked here that I can see, and you can't get through these islands except by way of the river. I'm guessing y'all didn't swim to the Watson

Place." He smiled broadly and asked, "Am I right?"

Ashley stayed silent, but Jack nodded in agreement. The man seemed nice enough, and he was just making sure the three of them were safe. People in Jackson Hole acted that same kind of friendly.

"Mosquiters eat you up yet?" the man asked.

"We're OK. We practically took a bath in bug repellent," Jack told him.

"Good idea." The man shifted his footing. "My name's Gordon," he said. "What's your name?" He was looking directly at Jack when he asked.

"I'm Jack, this is Ashley, and that's Bridger."

"Where y'all from?"

"Jackson Hole, Wyoming. How about you?"

"Oh, I'm from up north. Massachusetts. Well, you kids seem to be fine, so I'll be off, then. I'm fishing, too." He swept a tanned arm in the direction he'd come from.

Gordon's boat was about half the size of Frankie's, maybe only 17 feet from bow to stern, and it didn't have a cabin like Frankie's, just a white pilot seat midships and a bench in the stern. Jack didn't know a lot about boats, but he could see that this one had a powerful outboard motor, painted a deep, shiny blue that looked as though it had been buffed and polished just that morning.

"You guys had any luck fishing the Watson Place?" Gordon asked.

"No, not yet," Jack replied. "But we just started."

"Well, you gotta be patient. It'll happen." Gordon smiled, revealing straight white teeth that gleamed even whiter against his tan skin. "What are you using for bait?"

"Minnows," Bridger answered tersely. "Maybe you'd better leave before your motor scares the fish away from here."

Jack turned to stare at Bridger, surprised that he sounded so rude. He couldn't think of a reason Bridger was clamming up like that, not just untalkative, the way he was when he'd first met the Landons, but downright unfriendly. This guy Gordon had been nothing but nice. Maybe Bridger just didn't take to strangers. Whatever it was, his brusqueness didn't seem to bother Gordon in the least. The man kept his gaze fixed on Jack, as through the two of them were the only ones there.

"Looks like you have a nice camera. You taking lots of pictures of your trip?"

"You could see that from way downriver?" Jack asked, surprised.

"I have sharp eyes."

Jack couldn't make out the man's eyes at all, because he wore mirrored sunglasses, and the peak of his cap was pulled pretty far down. Only his nose really showed, sunburned and peeling. The rest of his face was covered by his neatly trimmed brown beard.

"You know, I'm interested in cameras," Gordon went

on, resting his forearms on the boat's rail. "I fish for fun, but my real love is pictures. I'm actually a professional photographer."

Ashley broke her silence to exclaim, "Really? Our dad's a professional photographer, too." Forgetting about not talking to strangers, she jumped to her feet. "Dad's been teaching Jack how to take good pictures with his new lens. It's awesome—he can shoot anywhere with it!"

"Wow—what kind is it?" Gordon asked, ignoring Ashley, directing all his attention toward Jack.

"Canon EF. 75 to 300 millimeter."

"Man, that's heavy duty. I was thinking about buying one of those babies myself. They're ranked as the best." Gordon moved closer, balancing easily even when the boat rocked in the water. "Mind if I have a look at it?"

Flattered, Jack took the camera out of the gear box. Holding it up, he said, "This lens cost me a lot of money."

"And he earned all of it himself," Ashley added. "Last winter he shoveled snow for everybody on our street."

"Ahhh, an entrepreneur." Gordon tugged at the peak of his baseball cap. "Can I have a look? It's different when you actually peer through a lens in the outdoors. You get a better feel for what it can really do. I'd like to give it a test drive before I buy, you know?"

"Uh...." Jack hesitated, because he didn't want to sound impolite, and yet he didn't really want to hand over his camera. "I—don't know...."

"I'll be careful, I promise," the man assured Jack, reaching out. When Jack hesitated, Gordon quickly jerked the camera out of his hands.

"Hey!" Jack cried.

"I'm just going to look," Gordon answered quickly. "That won't hurt anything."

Jack tensed. The air seemed to shift, as if the calm of the Everglades had turned threatening. Worried, he tried to figure out what to do next as Gordon moved around his boat, lifting Jack's camera in front of his face, peering in different directions.

"Give it back, OK?" Jack said, his voice low.

"This is great! I can practically see to Miami with this thing," Gordon exaggerated. "Let me check out one more view."

From the dock, Bridger's eyes were following Gordon's every move, the way the eagle had watched the osprey. Gordon kept changing his position in the boat, looking through the viewfinder from odd angles, ignoring Jack's outstretched hand. "Yeah," he said again, "it's exactly the kind of lens I want."

Unwinding his long frame, Bridger got to his feet. His jaw was set square, and his arms were crossed in front of his chest. The heels of his boots clicked hard as he strode forward. "My friend said to give it back. I suppose you ought to do that, mister. Right now."

"You're right. I suppose I should." Looking up, Gordon flashed a cool grin. "But I never was one to do what I should." In one fluid, pantherlike motion, he leaped to the steering wheel. As the motor roared, he gave Jack a wave with the back of his hand. This time, Gordon didn't worry about Bridger's fishing line. The propeller caught it and flipped the pole right into the water as the boat shot forward, leaving a V-shaped wake that cut the water like the tip of a sharp knife.

"Hey—my camera!" Jack yelled at the top of his lungs. "Give me my camera! Where do you think you're going?" He lunged toward the edge of the dock, but Bridger caught him and held him fast. Jack was so angry he felt as though his skin would split right off him, felt bile sting his throat, felt blood pound in his temples. If it hadn't been for Bridger, he might have jumped in the water to swim after Gordon and his fast speedboat. "Come back here!" he screamed, pulling against Bridger's strong arms.

"Give it up, Jack. He's outa here."

Too quickly the drone of the motor faded away, and in a moment, Gordon was gone. He never looked back.

"He took my camera!" Jack raged. "Why'd he—"

"He stole it," Bridger said. "There's thieves everywhere. He took you for a sucker, Jack."

"I'm not a sucker! He grabbed it right out of my hands!"

"You were showing it to him, some guy you've never even met before. What did you think was going to happen?"

"Jack—" Ashley began, but Jack ignored her. He was too furious with Gordon, and even more, with himself. He felt like he had to hit somebody, to vent his fury on something besides his own stupidity. It was bad enough that his camera was gone. It was worse that he'd just handed it over, like a little kid who didn't know any better. But Bridger had known. Right from the start, Bridger had figured out that Gordon was up to no good. For some reason, that made Jack even madder.

"Bridger, if you thought that guy was a crook, why didn't you say something at the beginning? Why did you let me keep talking to him like that?"

"I'm not your mother," Bridger snapped, color rising to his cheeks. "Besides, anybody with a brain in their head wouldn't go handing over something worth mucho dollars to a total stranger."

"Oh, so now you're saying I'm brain dead?"

"Yeah," Bridger said, pumping his fists so tightly that the veins bulged beneath his skin. "Dumb for trusting a stranger."

"Jack!" Ashley called again.

"Hold on, Ashley. I didn't hand it over, Bridger. He took it. Maybe I should have jumped into the boat and slugged him, maybe that's what you would have done, but that didn't seem like such a great idea at the time."

"Look," Bridger said, his tone softening, "I guess I'm just more careful 'cause I've seen a lot on the rodeo circuit. I learned the hard way."

"Jack, Jack," Ashley cried tugging on his shirt. "Pay attention to me."

"What do you want?" he yelled, so agitated he was stuttering. "I'm t-trying to deal with my camera. Don't bother me now."

It was Bridger who focused on Ashley's pale face, her frightened expression. "Hold it, Jack. What's wrong, Ashley?"

"Over there, swirling all around!" she said, pointing a shaking finger. "You see it? Right there!"

"See what?" Bridger asked, squinting toward where Ashley pointed.

"Blood. There's blood in the water!"

CHAPTER SIX

Before Jack could switch off his fury over the stolen camera, Bridger took off his hat, flung it onto the dock, then jumped into the water, boots-first. Everything was happening so fast, it was like an advanced level of a video game—too much action all at once, on all corners of the screen.

In the four-foot-deep water, Bridger waded to where Ashley said she'd seen blood.

"Right there," she called out. "No, a little more over that way."

"You sure?" he called back, gingerly feeling around with his foot. Then, "Oh-oh. Something down here. It's big—it feels like a body. Come on, Jack."

A body! That drove all thoughts of his camera out of Jack's mind; instead, he remembered Mr. Watson's cook. He hesitated, rocking on the toes of his sandals at the edge of the dock as Bridger urged, "Jack, get in here!"

Before Jack could move, Bridger submerged his whole head and torso under the mangrove-stained water. When he burst upward again in a spray of drops, he yelled, "It's a manatee."

"Dead or alive?" Jack jumped off the dock, splashing shoulder deep in the murky water. Just as he hit bottom, Bridger cried, "And it's got a baby."

"Wait for me!" Ashley landed right behind Jack. Since she was only five feet tall, the water came higher on her than on the two boys, all the way up to her neck. Instead of wading toward Bridger, she swam, her arms cleaving the ripples in precise strokes until she reached where Jack and Bridger were standing.

"OK," Ashley panted. Jack looked at Bridger, who gave a nod. "We'll do it together. Go," Bridger ordered.

The three of them plunged underwater at the same time. Even through the murk, they could see the huge, soft body of the manatee, with a baby tucked under her flipper. Bridger pointed at the manatee's back. It was slashed inches deep, like a hot dog split from the heat on a grill, and bleeding through the blubber beneath its skin.

When they burst above water for air, Jack cried, "The boat's propeller sliced her! Gordon killed her!"

"She's not dead," Ashley said, bouncing to keep her head above water. "The baby's nursing."

"But she's not moving. And she hasn't been up for air—a manatee can drown!"

Ashley shook her head. "They can stay underwater for 15 minutes, Mom said."

"Yeah, but any wild animal's gonna try to get away from people," Bridger told them, "and this one's just lying there. She's either cut too bad to move, or she's stunned from getting hit hard."

"Fifteen minutes...." Jack rubbed water out of his eyes. "That's the maximum. How many minutes since the boat slammed her?"

Bridger shrugged. "Don't know. Feels like a long time, but I can't really tell."

"We gotta bring her up for air," Ashley declared. "Or else she'll drown and the baby will die, too, without a mama to take care of it."

The two boys stared at her. "What do you mean, bring her up?" Jack asked. "How? She must weigh half a ton, at least. Maybe more. She's *big!*"

"Everything weighs less underwater, Jack. You know that. I bet you two guys could get her head up so her nose is above water. You pull her, and I'll take care of the baby."

"But half a ton! No way!" Jack was sure it wouldn't work, and Bridger looked just as doubtful.

Ashley's hair was plastered to her face in dark fingers; she yanked the strands away from her eyes impatiently. "If we don't at least try, the mother manatee will die," she said, her brow furrowed in worry. "Then the baby will die. Do you want to just stand here and watch?"

"Maybe you're right," Bridger said slowly. "I've been around animals all my life, and I can tell this one's not acting right."

From his mother's research, Jack knew how valuable every manatee life was in the Everglades. If they did nothing, two more would die. Two more endangered lives lost, gone forever, like water into sand. Ashley's plan was impossible, but Jack couldn't think of anything better. Bridger's eyes flicked from Jack to Ashley, then back to Jack again, letting him make the decision. "OK, Ashley, it's worth a try," Jack agreed.

Bridger took a deep breath. "Let's do 'er, then," he said. Once again the three of them splashed beneath the still surface, and Jack felt the water, warm and dark, close over his head.

Jack and Bridger dove to the shallow bottom, swimming one on each side of the manatee, from its head to its flat, round tail. It lay motionless on the soft mud. Jack had known that manatees were big, but close up, this one looked enormous, shaped like a miniature submarine, 10 feet long at least. His father had said manatees were related to elephants, and Jack could see a resemblance—here and there, stiff, straight hairs grew out of its thick gray brown hide. Even its baby was huge, almost as long as Ashley was tall. How Ashley could possibly manage to get that big manatee calf up to the surface, Jack had no idea.

When the three of them came up for air again,

Bridger said, panting, "Running out of time. All I can figure to do is, you grab it on one side, Jack, under its flipper, and I'll take the other side. We'll try to heave her head up, nosefirst. Can't manage more than that. That thing's heavy as a full-grown bull."

"OK. If we just get the nose up, she can breathe," Jack agreed. Down they went again. The boys attempted to grab underneath the manatee's flippers, but their hands kept sliding off its rough skin. In all the commotion, the manatee calf separated from its mother; Ashley was able to wrap her arms around it. Moving in a swarm of bubbles, she lifted the calf to the surface just as Jack and Bridger came up for air.

The four-foot-long baby wiggled and began to squeal and squeak. Even if it was brand-new, it knew this wasn't supposed to be happening to it. "It's all right, baby, don't be scared," Ashley cooed. The 60-pound calf writhed in her arms, splashing water into Ashley's open mouth. "Puft!" she spat.

Suddenly, next to them, the water parted; they could feel it swirling around them, an onslaught pushing against them, before they even saw what caused the upheaval. An immense mass rose with a force that knocked Jack and Bridger off their feet. It was the mother manatee, looming huge, rivulets streaming off her gray sides, like in a scary movie where a sea monster emerges from the bottom of the ocean.

Even though she'd been hurt, the manatee's consciousness must have been penetrated by her calf's cries. Like any mother, she was rushing to defend her infant. Ashley barely managed to hang on to the calf. It squeaked even louder than before, while its mother answered with vocal squeals of her own.

"Drop the baby!" Bridger yelled. "*Drop it!*" When Ashley let the calf go, it swam to its mother's side.

Mouth agape, Jack stared into the adult manatee's face—wide-set, beady eyes, bristly moustache, a snout like an armored tank, ready to run over him. When she opened her nostrils to breathe, they looked like the finger holes in a bowling ball. Even though he knew that manatees were the gentlest of creatures, the animal's very size took Jack's breath away. "Let's get out of here!" he shouted, pushing himself backward through the water, trying to stay on his feet.

"Wait!" Instead of moving back, Bridger went closer to the manatee. "I want to get a look at those cuts. Find out how bad they are." But before he could get near, the manatee submerged again, her baby once more at her side. "I'm going back down," Bridger said, and followed the manatee beneath the surface.

"That Bridger—he's not scared of anything," Ashley said. "He's got guts, don't you think?"

In reply, Jack spit out a mouthful of water, not liking the taste of it.

Exploding through the surface, Bridger shook his hair so that drops flew in an arc around his head like beads of glass. "We're OK," he gasped. "I got a good look—the propeller just cut through skin and blubber on her back. Didn't go too deep."

"Is she moving?" Jack saw the ripples swirling only feet away from him. The manatee must be there, hidden by the murkiness.

"She's pretty much staying put. I think she's still stunned. The boat hit her hard."

"How bad is she bleeding?" Ashley asked.

"Not that much." Bridger pinched his nose, squeezing water out of his nostrils, then rubbed his eyes to clear them. "I think some of the blood's from giving birth. Looks like that baby was just born. Probably right before the big one got hit."

"I hope you're right—that she's OK," Jack told him. "When Frankie gets back, she can radio the park rangers. They might want to take the manatee some-place to heal."

Ashley bit the edge of her lip. "Except, how will the park people find her? She might swim away from here. Frankie said the pelican would get infected from just having a torn place in its beak. What'll happen with all those cuts the manatee has?" Jack didn't have an answer, but Ashley's face quickly cleared as she hit on her own plan. "I know. We'll circle her, the three of us, stand-ing around her so she can't get away. We'll use our bodies to keep her close to the shore."

"That's insane," Jack argued. "We can't stand here

in the water for hours, waiting for Frankie and then for animal rescue people to come." Anyway, he thought, three kids weren't going to make a half-ton manatee stay where it didn't want to be. He wiped the lens of his waterproof watch with his thumb. Ten forty-five. Frankie ought to be getting back soon. Shielding his eyes with his hand, he searched the waterway, looking for any sign of the *Pescadillo*. The glassy river was empty as far as he could see, shimmering in the sun as though it had been sprinkled with bits of mirror. Then a movement, barely breaking the water's skin, caught his eye. Twenty feet away something skimmed the surface. Immediately he remembered the big alligator that had been sunning itself on the sand-covered tangle of mangrove roots.

"We'd better get back on the dock," he said. "There's gators around here."

"But what about the manatee?" Ashley asked.

Squinting, Jack tried to understand the shape as it glided closer. The shape didn't look anything like an alligator. A fin, silver in the sun, sliced the water like a razor. A dolphin?

No! Suddenly, Jack realized what it was, out there in the water, and it made his throat clamp tight. "Ashley," he croaked. "Get out!"

"But—"

"Shark! Bridger, right behind you!"

With a splash, Bridger whipped around, his eyes

widening with fear when he saw the fin, now only five feet away from him.

"*Ashley, get out!*" Jack screamed again.

He felt as though he were in one of his nightmares, the kind where he tried to run but his legs felt as heavy and unwieldy as lead. Right, left, right, left—with every step he could almost feel teeth slice into his extended leg. Jack pushed through the water, holding his arms out as he pumped toward his sister, reaching for her. *Why did she seem so far away? Why was it taking so long to get to her?* Faster and faster he went until he grabbed her outstretched hand. Pulling her behind him, he reached the dock and heaved himself onto it, then leaned down and yanked Ashley straight up out of the water. Her shins scraped against the rough wood as she fell to her knees.

Bridger catapulted himself onto the dock, a sheet of water tumbling off his torso like a waterfall. "Did you see it?" he asked.

Ashley couldn't speak; she could only nod.

The three of them sprawled on the dock, gasping as they watched the fin circle the spot where the manatee had been only moments before.

"The shark's going after the manatee and her baby," Ashley said, her voice shaking.

Grim, Jack nodded. "Probably drawn by the smell of blood." They sat for a moment, staring, as the shape glided close, then farther away, like a phantom. Ashley drew her knees to her chest and thrust her chin on top, clutching her legs so tightly the skin on her fingers blanched white. Jack couldn't tell whether she was crying or whether the drops running down her cheeks were dripping from her hair. "We can't just sit and watch the baby get eaten," she whimpered.

Jack pointed in the direction of the circling shape. "Ashley, look at that thing—it's six, maybe seven feet long. One bite could take off a limb. There's nothing we can do."

"Maybe there is," Bridger said quietly.

Moving quickly, he flipped open the cooler and grabbed two six-packs of soda pop. "How good's your aim?" he asked Jack, thrusting a cold can into Jack's hand.

"Pretty good," Jack answered. "Ashley's, too. Why?"

"OK. Let's see if we can scare that thing away. Ashley, here's one for you. On the count of three. One...."

Jack cocked his arm. The silvery shadow was still circling, close to the dock, then farther out, then back again.

"Two...."

He tried to anticipate how fast the shark was moving. Aiming for the fin, Jack targeted the water just ahead of the shark's nose. By the time the can sailed through the air, it might make impact.

"Fire!"

Three cans of soda pop sailed into the river, but only one, Ashley's, came close to hitting the shark. Ashley's can grazed its back, but the shark kept moving, its circle tightening.

"Again!" Bridger barked.

Three more cans arced through the air. Three more hit with a big splash, but it was obvious that the water slowed the impact too much. The cans sank slowly, uselessly, to the bottom.

"Again!"

"It's not working!" Ashley cried. "The shark doesn't care, and for sure it's not swimming away!"

"We need something else," Jack said, looking around for something heavier, or sharper, that he could throw. If he'd been in Jackson Hole, he could have found plenty of rocks, but here, at the Watson Place, there were only leaves and silt. Feeling powerless, he watched the shark make another pass. He tried not to picture the baby manatee ripped by the shark's fierce teeth, or the mother being torn at the site of her wounds.

Ashley pounded her fist into her thigh. "We can't let the manatee die. We *saved* her."

"You're right." Without another word, Bridger grabbed Jack's fishing pole. With a cannonball splash, he jumped into the water, his hand clutching his pole above his head like a sword. "Go! Get out of here!" he cried, smacking the fishing pole into the water.

For a moment, Jack stood frozen, unable to believe that Bridger was risking his life. "Bridger—are you crazy?" he yelled.

"Animals are afraid of people," Bridger hollered back. "You've got to show 'em who's boss. Like bustin' a bull."

"Get out! It's not worth it!"

With a whiplike motion, Bridger beat at the water. The shark's attention was drawn to Bridger; instead of leaving, it moved closer. Its back barely skimmed the surface.

"Yeehaw!" Bridger screamed, hitting the bull shark squarely on the nose. "Git!"

"I'm going to help him—" Ashley began, rising to her feet.

"Like heck you are!" Jack grabbed her arm, pulling her back onto her bottom. "*No!*"

"Let go of me, Jack. I said, *let go!*" She tried to wrench her arm free, but Jack held on tight. There was no way he could let his sister go into such deadly waters. If anyone was going to help Bridger, it ought to be Jack, but if he joined the watery battle, he knew Ashley would be right behind him. No, he had to stay and keep his sister safe. There was a line between bravery and stupidity.

Bellowing, "Get outa here, you ol' shark," Bridger smacked the water, again and again, hollering cowboy-sounding cries that rose up into the mangrove forest, where screeching, cawing birds joined the racket. It was no wonder Jack missed the sound of the motor. Frankie's boat was rounding the bend.

CHAPTER SEVEN

So all the way back in the boat," Ashley went on, rubbing a hotel towel through her freshly washed hair, "Frankie kept saying, 'What are your parents going to think of me, letting you kids get into so much trouble?' And we told her it wasn't her fault. 'Cause, honest, Mom and Dad, Frankie told us we were supposed to stay put at the Watson Place. Which we did, sort of, except we went into the water right in front of the Watson Place— and for sure, Frankie would never expect that we'd do that—"

"That's right," Jack added. "She just wanted us to be able to fish instead of going all the way back to the ranger station with the pelican—"

"Stop!" Steven raised his hand, palm forward. "We're not blaming Frankie, not in the least. And we understand what you kids were trying to do with that manatee. You were trying to be helpful. Brave."

"Absolutely," Olivia agreed, looking around at Jack, Ashley, and Bridger. The five of them were clustered in Steven and Olivia's worn motel room, which had been scrubbed clean for so many years the linoleum seemed almost transparent. A round table, topped with fake wood, had been plunked into one end of the room where Steven and Bridger sat. Olivia and Ashley were perched on one of the queen-size beds, while Jack sat cross-legged on the other.

"Really brave," Olivia went on. "You saw the manatee injured, and its baby, and you did everything in your power to try to save them. What you need to understand is that the three of you did everything exactly—"

Jack was nodding, pleased that his parents understood and approved.

"—wrong," Olivia finished.

Ashley dropped the towel, her dark, wet hair as tangled as the mangrove roots. Bridger, who'd been sprawled in one of the green vinyl chairs, suddenly pulled himself up, as stiff and straight as if his back had been glued to a board.

"What?"

"You three did everything exactly wrong," Olivia repeated.

"I don't get it. Do you mean," Jack asked slowly, "the part about going in the water with the shark?" He hoped that was all his mother was talking about. But Olivia shook her head no.

"I mean all of it. I know you were trying to help, but you need to learn a few things about the manatees. For one thing, there's a law, called the Marine Animal Protection Act, that prohibits anyone from even touching a manatee. You tried to lift that mother manatee to the surface. Even though your intentions were good, you were breaking the law."

"Are they going to arrest us?" Ashley asked, wide-eyed.

"No, no, no," Olivia answered quickly. "No one's coming after you. I just want you to understand the reason that law was passed. Human contact stresses the animals really badly."

"You may not think so, but that manatee would have managed OK without you," Steven told them. "Instead, you three must have almost given that poor thing a heart attack."

For a moment it was quiet enough to hear the straining of the air conditioner, which clicked and whirred as it tried to cool the small room. Stone-faced, Bridger studied his damp cowboy boots. He seemed as deflated by Steven's words as Jack was. Maybe more, because during the entire boat ride back, Ashley had babbled on and on about how incredibly awesome Bridger was, and how cool he'd been to fight for the manatee.

Bridger leaned forward, his fists on his knees. "What about the shark? You sayin' it would have been better to let that thing eat the baby manatee?"

"Yeah, right. What about the shark?" Ashley agreed. "Sharks are bad. I hate them."

"Whoa, now, wait just a minute. There are no bad animals, just animals with different jobs to do," Steven stated. From his day in the sun, his face had been burned to a red gold, making his blue eyes even more startling. "Every link in the food chain has a right to be there. Even the shark."

"Absolutely." Olivia nodded. "But more important is the fact that the shark would have left that manatee alone. They don't eat manatees. In fact, manatees have no natural enemies, except, of course, humans. What I'm trying to say is that the shark wasn't interested in the manatee—it was interested in you."

"Us?" Ashley squeaked.

"Yes. You kids were actually drawing the shark to the scene. Every time you smacked the water, the shark got more and more interested. Sharks' sensors detect movement, so noise and commotion attract them."

Jack felt his stomach sink. He'd thought—well, it didn't matter what he'd thought; he'd been wrong. They'd botched the manatee rescue, and worse, Bridger had risked his own life for nothing.

"Wow," Ashley said, flopping backward on the bed, her eyes searching the ceiling. With her knees bent toward him, Jack could see the scrape marks the rough dock had left, like a starburst of scabs on her skin.

"That shark would have been long gone except for

the fact that you kids kept harassing it. And Bridger"—Olivia's voice turned sharp—"getting into the water was about as foolish a thing as you could have done. Most sharks are actually timid, but Frankie said the one you tangled with was a seven-foot bull shark. She got a good look at it when her boat chased it away."

"The most cantankerous shark in the Everglades, and you take the animal on," Steven told Bridger, his voice low. "What you did was not only extremely dangerous, it was foolhardy."

"Yes, sir," Bridger said stiffly.

"Never assume that because you understand how one animal behaves, you can figure out another. A bull shark is nothing like a bull. You could have paid a big price for your heroics, Bridger. Do you understand?" Steven's eyes narrowed, but at the same time, he reached his hand across the table and rested it on top of Bridger's.

"Yes, sir, I do." Steven's hand was there only an instant before Bridger pulled away.

"Well, then, let's all go get some dinner," Steven said, his voice lightening. "Bridger, your boots look pretty soaked. I have an extra pair of sandals. Want to borrow them?"

"No, sir." Bridger shook his head.

At dusk, Everglades City lit up like a small jewel. Olivia decided that since the restaurant was only a few blocks away, and the night was crystal clear, they should walk to dinner. Everyone agreed except Bridger, who said nothing. He hadn't spoken much at all after the discussion about the shark.

Even though the air conditioners in their motel rooms were ancient, they'd done their job well enough to make the outside air feel shocking. It was as though Jack had stepped into a sauna. The heat made them walk slowly along the dirt walkway: Olivia, Steven, and Ashley in front, Jack and Bridger in the rear.

Tiny stores dotted the main road, their windows glowing from lights inside that made them look friendly. Beside one of them, Jack paused and pretended to look through the glass at some comic books on a display rack. Tugging Bridger's arm, he whispered, "Hey, hold up a minute. What's wrong?"

"Nothin'." Bridger hardly slowed down.

Hurrying to catch up, Jack asked. "You sure? Come on. You can tell me."

Bridger turned his head halfway for a quick glance at Jack, as if deciding whether it was worth answering. "OK," he said, "it's just—"

"Just what?"

"Frankie trusted me, and I screwed up." He kept walking, hands in pockets, staring down at the path in front of him.

"Hey, Bridger, it's not your fault. You didn't know about sharks and manatees. I didn't, either."

"But I was in charge."

Through the rest of the walk, Jack tried to persuade Bridger not to blame himself, but Bridger just clammed up and kept shaking his head.

"Here's where we're going to eat," Steven called back. "Right there." The Captain's Table Restaurant hovered against the water's edge. As the five of them made their way toward the carved wooden doors, a swarm of mosquitoes covered them like a black mist.

"They're in my hair!" Ashley cried. "Jack, there's a bunch of them on your back." Bridger swatted his cowboy hat through the air, while Steven smacked at his own neck with loud slaps.

"These are awful!" Olivia said, yanking open the door and hurrying the rest of them inside.

A plump woman, her pale eyes lined with indigo blue, greeted them with a knowing smile. "Welcome to the Captain's Table. Skeeters got ya, huh? Here in the Everglades, we consider the mosquiter our state bird. In the old days, houses had a skeeter room where people could brush them off so they didn't drag the critters through the rest of the house, but we don't have rooms like that anymore." She gave a light laugh, then ushered the Landons and Bridger around a corner and into the main dining hall.

The feeling of phantom mosquitoes on his skin made Jack itch all over, even though he knew nothing was on him, and even though he wasn't the one mosquitoes usually feasted on. Imagine needing a special room in your house to debug yourself! He was just deciding he would never want to live in a place like Everglades City when he noticed the restaurant's wall of glass windows, with the sun setting behind them.

A blazing ball of gold burnished a sky streaked with bronze and amber, and lit waves that looked as if a giant brush had been dipped in glitter and then painted across the horizon. Luminous colors sparkled in a pattern of light and dark, moving and shimmering, while boats bobbed at the pier, their masts cutting into the sky like church spires. Palm trees thrust dark silhouettes against the rosy dusk—the whole scene took Jack's breath away. Suddenly, a few bug bites in exchange for this spectacular view seemed a small price to pay.

"I'll sit you right by the windows so you can watch the sunset," the woman said, handing them their menus. "Enjoy your dinner, folks."

Jack couldn't be bothered to read the menu, not with this beauty in front of him. If only he'd had his camera, he could have captured the spectacular scene on film. The thought made his chest ache.

"What's the matter, Jack?" Olivia asked. "You look like you're ready to—"

She was probably going to say "cry," but caught herself in time so she wouldn't embarrass Jack in front of Bridger.

"I was thinking about my camera being stolen."

"Oh. Well, I told you insurance should cover it, honey. What a day you kids had—first a thief, then a manatee, then a shark!"

Steven unrolled his linen napkin and set his silverware to the side of his plate. "You know, I think the part about that man stealing your camera was the strangest of all. I don't think there's much chance of finding him. How low can you get, stealing from a kid?"

"Bridger tried to tell Jack not to hand over the camera to the man, but Jack did, anyway," Ashley said. "Huh, Bridger?"

Bridger's voice was flat. "I guess."

Jack looked out the window, then back to his parents. "He had an expensive boat—it's not like he couldn't afford to buy a camera. I don't understand why he took mine."

"There's no telling with people," Steven explained. "It's like with the shark: You think you can figure it out by just looking at the situation, and then—wham! You find things are not what they seem. That's the way life is. Sometimes you just don't know." Maybe Steven wasn't intentionally directing that at Bridger, but it wouldn't have mattered anyway. Bridger's eyes were locked on his fork. He plucked one of the tines with his thumbnail as if he were picking a string on a guitar. Plink, plink, plink. If this had been a movie, Jack thought, the sound track would have started up right then with one of those gloomy cowboy songs.

What right did Bridger have to mope? It was Jack who'd lost his prized possession. He was so caught up in his own unhappiness that at first he didn't tune in to what Ashley was saying.

"...and he said he was fishing, but there wasn't any fishing pole in his boat, or any fish, or bait, 'cause I looked. And another thing I looked at—you know how boats have numbers painted on the side? Well, this one had FL and then a 10, and I don't remember the rest."

Steven spread out his napkin on his lap. "Too bad you don't. But you couldn't be expected to remember. There'd be too many numbers and letters."

"But I remember the name on the motor," Ashley said. "Mercury. That's what it said. Mercury."

"Thanks for trying to play detective, Ashley," Jack told her, "but 'Mercury' is on half the outboard motors around here. But hey—" He gave his sister a little punch. "You're *good!*"

Ashley accepted the compliment as if it were her due. "I noticed this, too," she said. "That man said he was from Massachusetts, but he sounded more like the people around here."

"What do you mean?" Olivia asked.

"Well, he said 'y'all.' And 'mosquiters' instead of 'mosquitoes.'"

"That doesn't count for much," Steven commented. "You can't tell where someone's from just by hearing a couple of words."

"What else?" Jack asked, alert. "Tell me more."

Encouraged, Ashley went on, "He had one of those really expensive watches. A Rollo-dex."

"You mean Rolex," Olivia said.

"Whatever. And something else—his beard was a different color than the hair on his arms."

Now all of them were staring at her.

"I mean, his arm hairs were real blond—really, really blond—and his beard was kind of a dark brown. Well, he couldn't fake his arm hairs, could he? But he could have faked a beard."

"Ashley...." Steven's tone was skeptical. "All this sounds pretty wild. Fake beards? Why would anyone—?"

"'Cause with the hat and sunglasses and his beard, we couldn't really see his face. He didn't want us to."

Steven just shook his head.

"Dad, how come you never believe me?" Ashley asked. "Jack does, but you don't."

"I believe her, too," Bridger said, low. "Well, maybe not the beard part, but everything else Ashley said is right. About us not seeing his face, and about him having money. I've seen lots of rich guys when the rodeo goes to Las Vegas. They wear watches like that. This guy had a big gold ring, too. And the sunglasses—that kind of sunglasses costs mucho bucks."

Olivia frowned. "So why would he steal Jack's camera?"

Steven declared, "It doesn't make sense, that's for

sure. But here's what I'm thinking. The camera's gone, and we're getting some pretty far-out theories being raised around here. So how about if we just quit worrying about it for tonight and enjoy our dinners."

Jack tried to study the menu, but his brain was buzzing with everything he'd just heard. All of them were subdued when the food arrived, although Olivia and Steven made an attempt at pleasant conversation.

"I've got to get back to the room and do some work," Olivia announced when she finished eating.

"I'll walk you back," Steven told her, "and then I'm going to the one-hour photo lab up the street—it's open till nine. I want to develop the film I shot today."

"I want dessert, please," Ashley announced.

"Why am I not surprised? What about you two?" Olivia asked Bridger and Jack.

Bridger nodded, and Jack said, "Sounds good. Dad, I left a roll of film on the dresser in my room. Would you get it and have it developed with yours? Here's the room key."

"Sure thing. You guys take your time and enjoy your dessert. I'll pay on the way out, so you can stay as long as you want."

The last vestiges of the sunset had faded when the waitress brought Ashley's chocolate sundae, Bridger's apple pie à la mode, and Jack's key lime pie, which the waitress said was the specialty of the house.

Through the large windows, they looked out at the

Everglades City dock. At the far end, a small tour boat was moored, but since it was almost nighttime, all the tours were over until the next day.

"You want to go back to the motel?" Jack asked when they finished their desserts.

"Not really," Bridger answered.

"Me neither," Ashley said.

Jack looked around the room. "There's lots of empty tables, so we're not taking up space, like if someone else was waiting for a table."

Bridger nodded. "So?"

"So let's talk. Why did that guy take my camera?"

With the tip of his knife, Bridger drew circles on the tablecloth. "He liked your lens, and he didn't want to go buy one."

"Lame," Jack said.

"I know."

"He's a mean psychopath and he hates kids," Ashley ventured.

"That's a lame reason too, Ashley."

"So, OK, genius, what do you think's the reason?" Jack shrugged. "I don't have a clue."

With her index finger, Ashley wiped chocolate sauce from the inside of her dish, then licked her finger.

"That's gross," Jack told her.

"No one's watching. Besides, who are you anyway, the dessert police? We're not supposed to waste stuff, and chocolate is a natural resource." A smile crinkled the edges of her lips as she took another fingerful and stuck it, dripping, into her mouth. "Mmmmm, look, Jack. Yummy. Want some?"

Jack gave his sister a withering glance.

Bridger must have thought Jack and Ashley were building up to a real fight—which they weren't—because he broke in with, "Are you getting your pictures developed 'cause you took one of Gordon and his boat?" Bridger asked Jack.

He shook his head. "Wish I had. I was just snapping birds."

Bridger stretched out his long legs and sighed. He was wearing that faraway look again.

"What are you thinking about?" Jack asked him.

"Home in Montana. My dad in the hospital. Why I'm wasting time here with you."

The words stung Jack, but he kept his voice guarded. "Wasting?"

"I didn't mean it that way. Guess here's as good as any place for now."

Ashley, always the one to coax things out of people, didn't seem offended. Instead, she smiled and asked quietly, "Is it hard being with us—I mean, since we're almost strangers?"

"Not hard, exactly. It's"—Bridger rubbed his chin, as if trying to loosen the words from his mouth—"I reckon it's the way your family's different than mine. My dad would have told me that trying to protect something weaker, like the manatee and her baby, is always a good thing. My dad would have called me a man for trying."

Jack couldn't think of any way to answer that, so he stayed silent. He did think about what a contradiction Bridger was. Only yesterday Bridger had stated that "people are people, critters are critters," as if the critters didn't matter too much. And he'd teased Ashley about being afraid to hurt a fish's feelings. Yet he'd risked his life to try to save a manatee. Which was the real Bridger?

"Are you going to be a rodeo king like your father when you get older?" Ashley asked.

"Yeah, that's my dream. I want to start riding in the bronc-busting events right now, but Dad says I have to wait till I'm 16."

Ashley's questions seemed to have mellowed Bridger, pulling him out of his somber mood. Jack joined in and began to quiz him about the rodeo. Bridger answered easily enough, telling where the horses and bulls came from, who were the youngest riders on the circuit, who'd won the most championships in the different events.

Full from his dinner and the key lime pie, Jack leaned back in his chair and listened. The sound of dishes clattering in the kitchen ebbed and flowed with the opening and shutting of the kitchen doors, a back-drop to Bridger's soft, steady rhythm. The weight of the day pressed on him, and Jack felt his own thoughts slow to a crawl. Even though it was only eight o'clock, he was ready to head back to the room and go to bed.

For the last few minutes of their rodeo talk, Ashley had been staring through the window, her forehead pressed against the glass. Now she said, her voice hushed, "Jack, Jack! Look out there."

"What?" The tone of Ashley's voice snapped him to attention.

"At the wooden pier. See that? One, two, three, four slips down?" Wide eyed, she turned to stare at him. "It's the boat!"

"What boat?"

"Gordon's boat. It looks just like it."

CHAPTER EIGHT

Staring though the glass, Jack followed the direction of Ashley's finger. A boat, expensive and sleek, swayed gently in the sable waters. Instantly he recognized the craft. It belonged to the man who stole his camera.

"That's it for sure!" Jack cried. He was halfway to his feet when Bridger grabbed him and pulled him back into his chair. "Don't go getting all twisted into a knot. We've got to do this right," he hissed. "The man could be in here, right now, watching us. You look behind me, and I'll check out the tables behind you. But don't make it seem like you're looking."

Bridger was right, Jack knew, so with half-closed eyelids, he made a sweep of the few patrons still occupying the near-empty restaurant. An older couple held hands in the back corner, deep in conversation; a busboy with fuzzy blond hair stacked dirty dishes into a tub; and behind him, to the rear of the restaurant, two women lost in conversation stabbed at their salads. No man with a beard was anywhere Jack could see. Or without a beard, if Ashley was right about that.

"Clear in my direction," Bridger said. "How's it lookin' your way?"

"No sign of him. Look, my camera might still be in that powerboat. I want to get it back!"

"Then call the police," Ashley insisted.

"No." Bridger shook his head. "That boat could be gone before the cops made their way over here. Jack's right. Him and me'll check it out."

"And what am I supposed to do?" Ashley flared.

Standing slowly, Bridger bent his tall frame across the table. Leaning on his knuckles and leaning on every word, he told her, "You—stay—right—here. Got it? No telling what'll happen out there, Ashley, but one thing I do know is it's no place for a girl. I'd appreciate it if you'd sit here and be a lookout."

"I don't want to be a lookout—don't you remember what Dad said about the shark?" Ashley almost squeaked out the last word. "He told you that you shouldn't be stupid about doing dangerous stuff. This is dangerous. And stupid!" She turned to Jack, her eyes pleading, but Jack was too pumped to respond. The boat was there, less than 50 yards away. This might be his only chance to get his camera back. There was a time for words and a time for action.

Quickly he rose and stood next to Bridger. "Sorry,

Ashley, but I gotta do this. We'll be back," Jack said. And they marched out of the Captain's Table and into the night.

Directly in front of them was a small parking lot, guarded by a streetlight in one corner that illuminated the few cars parked there and lit a part of the pier at the water's edge. To their right, steps led to the pier; it was flanked by wooden pillars spaced every ten feet. A pelican balanced one leg on the nearest piling, its yellow eyes watching Jack's every move. As they approached, the bird spread huge wings as if to warn them off, but Jack hardly paid attention. The boat was only a few yards away.

"Do you think the guy's around here somewhere?" Jack asked, his heart picking up speed. "What are we going to do if he sees us?"

Bridger answered without hesitation. "Hope he does. I'd like to come up against that thief."

They passed a small canopied rig, then a boat hardly bigger than a canoe. Next came a sailboat with a 12-foot mast, one that gently wafted up and down in time to the water slapping the pilings. The next boat was the powerboat. After that came an empty slip where no boat was tied up.

Bridger craned his neck to see behind him. "We're OK. Everything's clear."

"Look." Jack pointed to the registration number on the bow. FL 10397 NK. "Like Ashley remembered."

The weathered boards of the pier creaked as they turned down the smaller finger pier dividing that slip from the one next to it. Gordon's boat bobbed beneath them, empty and lifeless.

"OK. I'll check it out," Bridger told Jack.

"No!" Jack said, surprised at how fierce his own voice sounded. "It's my camera. You stand guard."

Bridger didn't answer, but instead gave a sharp nod. Reaching down, he grabbed the line that tethered the boat to the pier and yanked hard; the boat sidled against the finger pier, bumping the wood with a soft thud.

After a final glance around, Jack jumped into the boat, arms spread-eagled until he steadied himself. The inside of this craft was different from Frankie's, smaller and more compact. Its fiberglass bow had a sharper point. At midship, a waist-high console held the steering wheel; behind it was a white vinyl pilot's seat. Everything seemed clean and polished, down to the stainless steel rail around the bow; it caught the faraway light like a strip of mirror.

"Find anything?" Bridger asked softly.

"No. But something's tied down over here. I'm gonna check it out."

"Hurry," Bridger warned.

A large white cooler had been pushed against one side. When Jack tried to open it, he couldn't get the lid to budge. On closer inspection he realized the clasp had been fastened with a small padlock. As he examined the lock, a slight odor drifted from the cooler, damp and a bit fishy; maybe the guy had gone fishing after all. Anyway, no one would stash a camera with a bunch of fish. He'd have to keep looking.

Slowly, Jack made his way toward the front of the craft, his hands skimming the sides as if they were etched in Braille. Now he was midship, where the padded white chair gleamed like a moon. Nothing was there, not on the console, not on the seat. No wrappers, no cans of soda, no navigation charts, nothing.

He was about to give up when his eyes caught a shadow within a shadow underneath the pilot's seat. Squatting low, Jack reached blindly into the darkness. His fingers touched something smooth and cool, then wrapped around a thin leather strap. His camera! He brought it up to his face, his heart pounding. There was just enough light to make out his special lens, a glass orb staring back at him.

"Bridger, I got it!" he cried.

Bridger was now hardly more than a dark silhouette on the finger pier. He pumped the sky with his fist. "All right!"

"Hey—the back of the camera's hanging open. He must have taken the film out. That was a fresh roll I put in."

"Forget the film. There's a couple of people walking past the parking lot. Come on!" Bridger's voice was soft but compelling.

With his camera in one hand, Jack climbed onto the finger pier, flush with triumph. Gordon hadn't won. Whoever he was, he'd thought he'd bested Jack, but now Jack had done him one better and had beaten him at his own game. For a moment he allowed himself to imagine the man returning to his boat; he'd reach for the camera and find empty air. Jack wished he could see the expression on Gordon's face when that happened. Checkmate!

"Now we know for sure this boat belongs to the guy who robbed me," he told Bridger. "We need to call the police."

"Bet they arrest him." Breaking into a sudden smile, Bridger gave a high five, so hard Jack's skin stung. "You did it!" he said, his voice warm with admiration.

"Yeah," Jack agreed. "I did."

The night sky lightened as another streetlamp blinked on, this one at the farthest end of the dock. Golden light made a zigzag design in the marina waters, like lightning on black satin, and Jack almost laughed at the beauty of it. Now he could take a picture. First thing he'd do would be to get another roll of film, and then he'd be out trying to capture the Everglades night. He asked Bridger, "Do you think I can still make it to the photo shop for—"

But Bridger wasn't paying attention. "Wait. Shhh." He held his fingers to his lips, signaling Jack to be quiet. A scuffling sound, coming from the edge of the pier nearest the parking lot, broke the evening stillness. Footsteps. Bridger and Jack were still on the finger pier when a figure approached from the pier side, closing the gap between them before Jack and Bridger could escape. Jack stood, frozen, his eyes trying to make sense of the shadows. Maybe the man would walk past. There were a few other boats tied to the pier and a restaurant close by. He watched, his whole body on alert.

Sauntering, hands jammed into his jacket pockets, his jaw working as though he were chewing gum, the man slowed as he got closer to where Jack and Bridger stood. He stopped at the point where the finger pier jutted off the main pier, next to the empty slip. "Hey, kids. What's up?" he asked, cocking his head to one side.

Jack's stomach clamped. If this was the owner of the boat, they'd made a mistake, because he looked different from the guy named Gordon. He was clean-shaven, with white-blond hair combed off angular features.

"You want something?" the man asked again. "What are y'all doin' here?"

It didn't matter how altered his appearance was, Jack now recognized the voice. It was the man who'd stolen his camera. *Gordon*.

Coolly, Bridger said, "We were just checking out your boat. Looks fast."

"Faster than any of these other tubs. So why don't you get in, and I'll give you boys a ride."

"No thanks," Jack told him.

"What's your hurry? I'm thinking teenagers like you'd love a night ride."

Bridger shook his head. "Our folks are in the restaurant, waiting for us. They're watching us right now, from the window."

"Really?" Gordon made a clucking sound with his teeth. "I was just in there—had a drink at the bar. Place looked empty. So I guess they left you all alone." Gordon took a step closer. "Which is a good thing, 'cause now you can take a ride with me. No worries, right?"

Jack felt the hairs rise on the back of his neck. To his right was an empty slip, to his left, the powerboat. Behind him, more glassy water stretching into a tiny bay edged with palm trees. He looked to the restaurant for help, but from this vantage point he could see nothing except ceiling lights. The pier was empty. There was no one.

"You've got my camera, don't you." Gordon didn't ask it, he stated it.

"It's mine. *You* stole it from *me!*"

Gordon drawled, "That's quite an accusation. The way I see it, you got on my boat and took my property. Y'all are nothing but a couple of punk thieves. I have a right to take you to the sheriff. So get in the boat."

"Why are you doing this?" Jack demanded.

"I think you know. If you don't—my mistake. In that case, you're just innocent casualties. But my guess is you know more than you're saying, and since in my business it's important to be"—he paused to choose his word carefully—*"discreet,* that means we're all going to take a nice ride together. Now let's get on with it."

"I'm not getting in there. No way," Jack declared.

"Oh, but I say you are." Pulling his hand from his pocket, Gordon produced a small black pistol. He held it close to his body, pressed against his hip. Jack knew Bridger had seen it too; he also knew that no one else in the parking lot, if anyone were there at all, would notice the drama unfolding on the pier.

"Back up, and get in the boat," Gordon said again. Every bit of civility had melted out of his tone; there was nothing left but menace, the slapping of the water, and the gun.

"Don't do it, Jack," Bridger said through tight teeth. "He can't shoot us out here, not on the pier."

"But I might. Do you really want to find out?"

Bridger's fists locked, hard-knuckled. "If I have to."

Though Jack's mind was working fast, every possibility came up flawed. If he jumped into the water of the empty slip next to where they were standing, Gordon could move out onto the finger pier and shoot him directly, like a target in an arcade. But he also knew that if he did what Gordon ordered and got into the boat, he'd be at the man's mercy. No way out! The phrase flashed though his brain, again and again, like a neon sign.

"Move it," Gordon barked, starting to step onto the finger pier.

In the deep, quiet darkness, Jack thought he saw movement. A tiny flick of a motion, and then stillness, appearing and then disappearing like a firefly. Had somebody figured out what was happening? Had Ashley called for help?

"Did you hear me, boy?"

"Well, yeah, I guess I do, but...." Jack stalled, trying to buy time. Suddenly a shadow broke free from the other shadows and cannonballed toward them. Before Gordon could even turn around, his arms shot into the air and whipped wildly. For a split second he tottered back and forth, clawing air with the hand that didn't hold the gun, until gravity got the better of him and he plunged sideways into the empty slip. The water churned as he surfaced, sputtering.

Where Gordon had stood, a small figure hung poised, hands still upraised from the act of pushing a man twice her size. Ashley.

"*Run!*" Bridger yelled.

CHAPTER NINE

The Everglades sheriff's office wasn't located in the town; they had to drive back to the main highway, to the Tamiami Trail intersection. Inside the building they saw two officers in gray uniforms, their shirts open at the neck. One looked up at the Landons and asked, "Can I help you folks?"

Steven cleared his throat. "This sounds strange, I know," he began, and hesitantly told the story about the man stealing Jack's camera at the Watson Place. By the time he got to the part about the kids finding the boat outside the restaurant, all the Landons, plus Bridger, were chiming in.

"So he had a gun and he told us to get in the boat," Bridger stated.

"And then Ashley pushed him in the water, and we ran away on the pier and I had my camera—" Jack added excitedly.

"Whoa, whoa, whoa—give me a minute here. Folks, you better sit down," the sheriff interrupted. He was young and dark-haired with sharp, dark eyes fringed with thick lashes, and a wide black moustache. "Tom, are you hearing all this?" he called to the deputy behind the counter.

"Uh-huh."

"Get the paperwork started, will you? Looks like we're gonna have to file a report."

"OK, Carlos."

The deputy named Carlos shepherded them to a long bench against the wall, then rolled up a desk chair on wheels and sat facing them. "Now, uh, Mr. and Mrs. Landon," he began, glancing at a slip of paper to make sure he had their names right, "what I'm hearing sounds pretty serious, so I'm going to have to get the information in an orderly way. I'd like to ask the kids a few questions, and I'm gonna ask you two grown-ups to let them answer. In other words, Mr. and Mrs. Landon, please refrain from talking, even if you think you have something important to say. You'll have your chance later. Right now I just want to hear from these kids."

Steven and Olivia agreed.

"OK, let's start again. First things first. Jack—it's Jack, right?"

Jack nodded, watching Carlos intently.

"Let's begin with you. You say you kids were out fishing at the Watson Place?"

"That's right."

"And what time was that?"

"This morning. We got there about 9:30."

"OK," Carlos muttered, writing the time down. "You were fishing, and then what happened?"

"This man came up and stole Jack's camera!" Ashley blurted out.

"That was later," Jack said. "Probably a quarter after ten."

"Ten fifteen," Carlos acknowledged. "The man took it, and then took off in his boat. Why do you think he would do that?"

"'Cause it was an expensive camera," Ashley babbled. "It was our dad's—he's a professional photographer— and then he gave it to Jack, and then Jack bought a new lens that cost a lot."

"OK, the motive was robbery. Let's go on. The man who stole the camera said his name was Gordon. Was that his first name or last name?"

Jack shook his head that he didn't know. Bridger muttered, "Probably wasn't his real name anyway."

"An alias." Carlos's pen scratched against the paper. "And you said he had a dark beard and sunglasses and a hat pulled down to his nose. Is that right? But the man you say pointed a gun at you on the dock at the marina didn't have a beard. So how could he be the same person?"

"Because he must have had a fake beard when he

was at the Watson Place," Ashley answered confidently. "He took it off before we saw him tonight."

"A fake beard? Is that right? A fake beard. Hmmmm."

Jack couldn't be sure, but he thought a tiny flicker of a smile twitched across the deputy's lips. Then he turned to Jack and Bridger again. "I've got another question for you. Why do you think the boat at the Watson Place and the boat in the Marina were the same boat?"

"For one thing, they looked exactly alike, plus both boats had the same registration—at least the beginning numbers. FL 10. That's what Ashley remembered from this morning—FL 10. She couldn't remember the rest, but the boat at the pier had FL 1039—uh, 7—N—something, on it."

"NK," Bridger said.

"I was thinking it was NL. But I'm not sure," Jack admitted.

"NK, or maybe NL." Carlos made more notes, then leaned backward in the chair, causing it to squeak. "How much did you say that camera was worth?"

"A lot. Why?" Jack asked impatiently.

"I'm just trying to get at a motive." Carlos raised his thick black eyebrows. "What do you think this Gordon was going to do with you two? Seems like an awful lot of risk, just for a camera. Even if it was expensive."

Something was wrong here, Jack could tell. It wasn't what Carlos was saying, but the way that he said it that made Jack think the deputy wasn't convinced by their story. Jack shifted uncomfortably in his seat. Up to that moment, he hadn't realized how farfetched the whole thing really sounded.

"Let me clarify. A man wearing a fake beard brings his boat all the way over to the dock you're fishing on, and then steals your camera. Then, later on, you find the boat and take your camera back. But before you can escape, this Gordon catches you, only this time his beard is gone. He threatens you with a gun and tells you to get in his boat. Do I have it right so far?"

The kids nodded.

The deputy crossed his arms, looked at Jack, Bridger and Ashley, one after the other, and said, "Before we go any further, you need to be sure you're telling me the absolute truth. No making up anything."

"You can believe what they're telling you. My children are trustworthy," Steven declared, an edge to his voice.

"I'm sure you believe they are," Carlos agreed, his eyes never moving off Jack's. "I just want them to understand something. They're starting up a police procedure here with their story, and it's real important that they be completely truthful." He paused, uncrossed his arms, and leaned forward to look intently at the three of them, one after the other. "I want you all to think about that for a minute. Only the truth, right? Now, is there anything else you want to tell me?"

"Everything we've told you is the truth," Bridger snapped.

Deputy Carlos sighed. "All right. Let's get back to the man with the gun. Now, it was dark, right? How could you be sure he was holding a gun?"

Shrugging, Bridger answered, "I've seen plenty of guns. I know what they look like."

"Then the girl—your name's Ashley, isn't it? Then Ashley pushed him into the water. How did you manage to push a full-grown man into the water like that?"

"I caught him off-balance. Hey—a dog can push somebody over if it jumps on them from behind, you know? You can knock anyone off-balance if they don't know you're going to do it and they don't see you coming. Besides, I'm stronger than I look!" When Carlos gave a half-smile, Ashley cried, "Stand up and turn around and I'll show you—"

Grinning now, Carlos said, "That won't be necessary."

Jack studied the scuff marks on the pale tile floor. He felt pretty sure that Carlos didn't believe them. Their story did seem bizarre, he realized. Still, he wasn't used to having his word doubted.

Bridger must have been thinking the same thing. As Deputy Carlos squeaked backward in his chair again, Bridger frowned and told him, "Look, I don't care how weird this sounds, we're telling you the truth."

"Right. But I'm wondering if you might have mistaken some of what you saw. For example, when you were at the marina, it was dark. Could it be possible that this Gordon fellow just pointed at you with his finger, like this"—Carlos cocked his hand—"and because you were scared, you thought it was a gun?"

The two boys shook their heads vehemently. "No," they said in unison.

Blowing a stream of air between his lips, Carlos told them, "The reason I'm hung up on this is I can't figure out why a camera would be worth that kind of risk. You say it's valuable, but is it that expensive? Worth kidnapping for?"

"I don't know, sir," Bridger said, his voice low. "He said he thought we knew something, but that if he was wrong, then that was too bad."

"Did you see him do anything illegal?" Carlos asked, leaning forward again. "When he approached you at the Watson Place, did you see anything unusual in his boat? Anything that might have made him nervous? When he came up to the dock, did you take his picture?"

"No, I was fishing." Jack studied the ceiling, replaying the scene in his mind, but he came up blank. Nothing about Gordon had seemed strange that morning, nothing in his boat out of place.

"You're not giving me much to go on," Carlos said, rising to his feet. "We'll need to keep the camera until we bring in this guy and investigate the facts."

"What!" Jack cried.

"I'm sorry, Jack, it's evidence. I'll run these boat registration numbers, see if we can dig up anything. That's the best we can do for now. In the meantime,

I'm going to need your folks to sign some papers, and then I'll send an officer down to the marina to look for that boat."

"It's not there," Steven said stiffly. "I already checked before we came here. The slip's empty."

"You should leave the police work to us, Mr. Landon. Write down the phone number where you're staying, and we'll keep in touch. I'm sorry we can't do more for you folks. We'll take this as far as we can."

"But—how long before I can have my camera back?" Jack asked.

"Oh, a day or two. It would help if you had some proof of ownership, like a sales slip or something. That would speed things up."

"All that stuff's back in Jackson Hole!" Jack protested.

"Sorry, fella. I have to go by the book."

Dejected, the kids walked out of the sheriff's station, Olivia and Steven behind them. "Don't worry, Jack," Olivia said. "As soon as we straighten this out, we'll get your camera back."

"It's not that," Jack said, and Ashley echoed, "Yeah, it's not that. What makes me mad is that they didn't believe us, at least all the way. I thought they'd call in the FBI and helicopters and stuff."

"I could tell just by looking at him that he didn't think it really happened the way we said it did," Bridger told them.

"It might have been the bit about the fake beard,"

Steven mentioned. "I think that's when you lost them, Ashley. It sounds too unbelievable."

"Oh, great!" Her chin slumped down into the neck of her T-shirt as she scuffled to the parking lot.

In the car on the way back, nobody said much, not even after they arrived at the motel. They had adjoining rooms with a doorway in between: Steven, Olivia, and Ashley in one room, and Jack and Bridger in the other. Only, for now, Jack had pulled Ashley into his own room, thinking it best to let his parents have some time to themselves—he knew they wanted to talk about what had happened. Through the half-open door, he could hear his father's voice, soothing and low.

"Olivia, it's OK. The kids are safe. That's all that really matters. I promise I won't let them out of my sight for a minute the whole rest of the trip." Springs on a bed squeaked, and he guessed his father was sitting next to his mom, circling his arm around her like he always did when she was upset. "You've got to take your mind off it. We've done everything we can. The rest is up to the police."

"How can I think about anything else? That man pulled a gun on my son!"

"Or maybe the officer's right, and they just thought they saw a weapon. Either way, we know for sure the man was a thief, so at the very least I'm glad he got a dunking. Our little Ashley's turned out to be quite a spitfire."

Ashley'd been sitting on Jack's bed, reading a motel

magazine about things to do in Florida. When she heard her father call her a spitfire, she looked up and grinned.

Bridger grinned back, and gave her a thumbs-up.

"You know, you didn't tell me how it went out in the field today," Steven was saying.

"Don't ask me to talk about manatees—"

"Sweetheart, you've got to. That's why they brought you here. There's nothing more we can do about our phantom camera thief, not tonight, but you can help out with the manatees. What happened today, after I left you?"

Olivia hesitated, then began to speak slowly, as though searching for words. "They...they found a male, near death and too sick to eat. I went and examined him."

"Do you know what's wrong with him?"

"No, and the biologists at the Natural Resources Center are just as baffled as I am. It's so strange, Steven. Water pollution levels check out fine, the food source is thriving, temperature's OK. It isn't anything obvious like red tide, which wiped out so many of them a few years back. This one's a real mystery."

Their voices rose and fell, and after a while Jack heard the tension melt from his mother's voice as she went over all the material she'd collected on the manatees' strange illness. Every once in a while, Steven asked another leading question, and Olivia would shuffle papers before coming up with a reply.

Bridger had been pretending not to listen, doodling with a pen on the little notepad next to the phone in the room. He had an odd look on his face, a bit puzzled over what he was hearing. It must be because he wasn't used to conversation between a husband and his wife. Bridger'd been motherless since he was five, living in a male world full of danger and daring, never experiencing life with two parents or being part of a family.

Steven kept talking to Olivia about her problems—if only someone could come up with a solution for Jack's problem! He'd been so excited to have his camera in his hands again, and now it was gone once more.

A little later, Steven walked into the boys' room, saying, "Here are your pictures, son." He dropped the envelope onto Jack's bed. "Come on, Ashley. Time to get some sleep."

"OK. Night, Jack. Night, Bridger. See you."

Ordinarily Jack would have leaped to look at his pictures, but he was so discouraged about his camera that he just stayed slumped in the green vinyl chair, the twin to the one in his parents' room.

In front of the air conditioner, Bridger was building some kind of pyramid with his suitcase. On it he'd stacked one of the drawers he'd pulled from the scarred dresser, a phone book, and a couple of towels to top it off.

"What's that for?" Jack asked.

Carefully, Bridger set his boots on the wobbly

structure, with the open tops pointing toward gusts from the air conditioner. "I need to dry these things out," he said. "They're starting to smell. Don't know if it's from the swamp water or my feet."

That struck Jack as funny. He began to laugh, and soon Bridger was laughing with him.

"Why don't you give in and wear sandals tomorrow?" Jack asked him. "Dad said he'd lend you a pair. If you keep wearing those boots, you're going to get jungle rot and your toenails will all fall off."

That set them off again, and when they quit laughing, Bridger said, "Wel-l-l-l, I just might. Borrow the sandals. Hey, how'd your pictures turn out?"

By then, Jack was ready to look at them. Carefully he took them from the envelope. Holding them by the edges, he examined each print, one by one. "Not bad," he said, "but not good enough for NATIONAL GEOGRAPHIC."

"Let's see." Bridger sat next to Jack on the bed. Imitating Jack, he held the pictures by the corners and studied them. "This is good, the one of the gator going after that bird."

"The anhinga."

"And you got a pretty good one here of the eagle and the osprey fighting."

"Yeah, but the one I like best is the last one on the roll. The great blue heron flying."

When Jack held it up, Bridger said, "Yeah. Good job." He yawned. "But I'm tired, so I'm going to sleep."

He peeled off his jeans and another, fresh plaid shirt he'd taken out of his suitcase when they returned from Frankie's boat that afternoon: one he'd put on after showering off the murky mangrove water. Flopping onto his own bed, Bridger fell asleep instantly, without saying good-night.

Even with the air conditioner going, it was too hot to sleep under a bedspread. Jack sprawled on top of the sheets, planning to replay in his mind all that had happened that day, hoping for just one more clue that would help him get his camera back.

Methodically, he tried to call up all the details he could remember, beginning with his first sighting of the man's boat.

The room was a comfortable temperature, not too hot and not too cold. Since the motel was out a ways from the center of town, there weren't any streetlights to shine through the windows, and the motel itself was very quiet. Jack tried to force himself to stay awake so he could think, but he couldn't fight it. Sleep overtook him.

Much later, he reared up in bed. It was still dark; he groped for his watch and read the luminous numbers: 3:37. At first he only saw the 37, because his thumb covered the 3. And something clicked in his brain.

That picture of the great blue heron flying was not the last one on the roll. There'd been another one of it landing in a tree. In one-hour photo labs, like the one where his dad had taken the film tonight, the automatic print machines were set up to print exactly 36 pictures from a roll of 36, or exactly 24 pictures from a roll of 24. But Jack always managed to squeeze an extra shot onto each roll. He always got 37 or 25 negatives, depending on what size roll he was using. Today, he remembered, he'd shot 37. The lab hadn't printed number 37, but it would be on the strip of negatives.

Cautiously, hoping he wouldn't wake Bridger, Jack turned on the little lamp on the stand between their twin beds. Carefully, he took the negatives from the envelope. There it was, the 37th, although it wasn't numbered, because film numbers stopped at 36.

Negatives are hard to read, and the bulb in the lamp probably wasn't stronger than 40 watts, but as he held it up in front of the light, he felt a stab of excitement.

There was the heron in the tree, and farther beyond it, the man in the boat. He was reaching out to one of the pilings he'd stopped beside. Not reaching straight out, but down, toward the water level. Netting a fish? No, Ashley had said there was no fishing gear in his boat.

Straining his eyes, Jack could barely make out that the man wasn't looking at what he was doing, but had turned to face the Watson Place. He must have seen Jack taking pictures. And whatever he was doing there at the pilings, he didn't want anyone to know about it. That's why he stole the camera. But Jack had already taken out the roll of film.

Three fifty in the morning now. Jack burned to tell someone, but he thought he shouldn't wake Bridger, or wake his parents, either. His mother was having enough trouble of her own, worrying about the manatee mystery. He'd just have to wait till morning. Excited as he was, he thought he'd never fall back to sleep.

He was wrong.

CHAPTER TEN

Jack tasted salt. A fine mist of Everglades water, carried by the wind, sprayed his lips as they traveled farther into the channel. The *Pescadillo* moved more quickly than it had the first time they'd ridden in it. The bow cut through wave after wave as Frankie, eyes squinting against the sun, pushed ahead with determination. She'd set a course for the one spot that might answer the questions Jack's photograph had raised and that might explain why Gordon had been willing to steal a camera and try to kidnap Bridger and Jack. They were on their way to the Watson Place, and this time Olivia and Steven were with them.

"I'm guessing drugs," Frankie said loudly. She had to speak up to be heard over the engine's roar, so each word had more space around it, as though she were talking in exclamation marks. "I've been thinking about it since you called me. What we saw in the photo might be some kind of drop-off point."

Olivia's expression clouded. Pulling on Steven's arm, she said, "Drugs? Steven, we've got the kids with us. Maybe we should turn back and let the police handle it."

Jack shook his head hard. "They wouldn't believe us, not without proof. Even when Dad showed them the picture this morning, they said it didn't look like anything suspicious. And Sheriff Carlos still wouldn't give my camera back."

"Jack's right," Steven agreed. "First, we need to see what, if anything, is out there. Then we can decide our next move."

Ashley didn't say a word, just held her stomach tight with crossed arms. She sometimes suffered from motion sickness, but now she seemed determined to fight it—today was too important. Bridger, too, was quiet, but Jack sensed there was another reason besides the rolling of the boat. Bridger looked deep in thought, trying to figure things out, oblivious of the flock of birds moving lazily across the mangrove treetops, landing in the foliage as lightly as butterflies.

Sliding further into the white vinyl deck chair, Jack looked into the endlessly blue sky and the clouds that brushed against it, and started to think things himself. His dad had taken his negative into the one-hour photo lab as soon as it opened, then brought back an enlarged photograph, an eight by ten.

"There's definitely something here," Steven had told them, studying the picture closely. "I'm not sure what

I'm looking at, but Gordon's doing something—do any of you kids remember this box thing in the water?"

Jack, Bridger, and Ashley had all shaken their heads no. "From where we were," Jack said, "it just looked like some posts sticking out of the river."

And that's what the police concluded when Steven showed them the picture. "Nothing unusual there," they'd said. "The guy's just stopped beside some pilings. But we'll keep checking on the boat, like we said we would."

After that the Landons and Frankie had decided, over the phone, to investigate things themselves, Frankie insisting that they leave as soon as they could meet her at the dock. "I've got a personal stake in this," she'd told them. "The kids were attacked on my watch. I'd like to hook this Gordon and reel him in."

And as soon as they met her, Frankie identified the object in the photo. "It's a water-monitoring device. Checks the water level and a few other things, like temperature and salinity. There are a number of them at different spots in the Everglades." Since then, all of them had been turning over and over in their minds what this mystery could possibly involve. And now, 20 minutes away from the Watson Place, Frankie had suggested it might be a drug drop-off operation.

Ashley unfolded herself and slowly made her way to the bridge deck, stopping next to the three adults. Since Bridger seemed lost in his own thoughts, Jack decided to join the others. Walking unevenly, he made his way to where they were.

The life jacket was too big for Ashley's thin body; the edge of it kept creeping up underneath her chin. It made her look like a turtle in an orange shell. "Mom," she called out, "I've been searching for the manatee mama who got hit. Do you think she's OK?"

Olivia answered, "I asked my manatee experts about her, and they said that after they got Frankie's radio message yesterday, they went right out to find her. They're monitoring her and her baby, and so far, both are doing fine." Reaching out a hand, she ruffled Ashley's hair and said, "The sad fact is, almost every adult manatee has scars on its back or tail fluke from being hit. It's so common that researchers use the scar patterns to identify individual manatees."

Shaking her head, Ashley groaned, "That's awful."

"I know. But until people are more careful, manatees will keep on getting cut and sometimes killed."

"I'm always careful," Frankie declared.

"What makes it even more serious," Olivia went on, "is that manatees take so long to make babies. The average manatee produces only ten babies in her whole lifetime, one every two or three years. All manatees are doubly precious, for themselves and for the few babies they'll produce."

"Do the manatees wear tracking collars, like the

wolves in Yellowstone?" Jack asked, thinking back to their trip to that park.

"Not collars. Sometimes belts with monitors are put around the narrow section of their tails, but most manatees aren't tagged, since it's quite a job getting anything on an animal that big. Usually they're just left alone."

Jack nodded, remembering how huge the manatee had seemed when he and Bridger had tried to lift it.

"If they don't wear monitors, then how do the researchers find them? I mean, look at how dark the water is—you can't see anything in it," Ashley mentioned, pointing to the tea-colored depths.

A smile crept across Olivia's face, and she gave a little chuckle. "Well, now, they use some very ingenious ways, one of which I'm sure you kids will find awfully funny. First of all, how do you think a manatee stays afloat when it wants to come up for air? Adult manatees can grow up to weigh 3,000 pounds. Don't you think they would sink?"

"Blubber!" Ashley guessed, just as Jack said, "I bet it's the air in their lungs. In pictures, those lungs are awfully big—they'd be like two great big balloons."

"Partly wrong. Good tries, but not completely correct." She looked from one face to the other, expectant, but Jack had no idea what she was after. Steven, who'd been listening from the bow, joined Olivia and said, "Come on, now, you're not telling the kids the how-do-manatees-stay-afloat story, are you?"

Giving Steven a playful tap on the chest, Olivia answered, "Hey, guy, don't get so uptight. It's perfectly natural, especially when you consider their diet. All they eat is plant material. They're total vegetarians."

"So, Mom, how do they do it?" Jack pressed, sensing a good story.

"Well, manatees have large intestines that are 60 feet long and 4 to 6 inches in diameter. Their vegetation-only diet puts a lot of gas in their gastrointestinal tracks. In fact, manatee guts may have three to four times the volume of gas in them that their lungs have, and it's all that gas that keeps them buoyant. Now," she said, wiggling her eyebrow, "isn't that interesting?"

"But I don't get what all that has to do with finding them," Ashley said, looking puzzled.

Pleading in mock horror, Steven cried, "No, Olivia, you're not going to tell the how-the-researchers-locate-the-manatee story!"

Frankie was already laughing as Olivia answered, "It's a legitimate scientific question. Ashley, the little bubbles you see coming up onto the surface of the water aren't from their lungs. Marine scientists actually use something called a hydrophone—it's an underwater microphone they put it into the water—and they just 'listen' for the manatees to...well...expel some of that gas that's filling up their guts. Amazing, but true."

"You mean they hear the manatees—"

"That's exactly what I mean." Olivia grinned, then added, "Hey, whatever works."

Ashley and Jack broke into a fit of giggles. Evidently Bridger had been listening, too, from back in the stern, because he looked like he was trying to hold back his laughter, and at the same time trying not to blush.

"Gross," Ashley said.

"Natural," Olivia answered.

"There's the Watson Place," Frankie announced, slowing the boat. "I'll pull close to the dock so you can see where all the excitement took place yesterday, but we won't stop."

"Dad, you have your camera," Jack said. "Take some pictures, will you? I'm definitely gonna want to remember this scene."

All of them stared at the Watson Place while Steven photographed it, using both zoom and wide-angle settings. "I guess the old Indian curse is still working," Ashley murmured. "It started because the earth was bleeding when hunters slaughtered the alligators and egrets. Then people died at the Watson Place, so their blood got spilled, too. After that, Mr. Watson's blood. And now the manatees are dying."

"But no one's slaughtering the manatees, Ashley," Steven commented.

Ashley blurted, "How do you know? Mom hasn't been able to find out what's killing them. Maybe some mean person who hates manatees—"

"Honey, that's silly," Steven said, shaking his head. Olivia looked thoughtful, though, for a moment, as if she were considering something she might have missed before. Then she, too, shook her head.

"Well, we've visited the scene of the crime," Frankie announced, "so let's go find out what our friend Gordon was up to." Pushing the throttles forward to bring the boat out of idle, she quickly covered the short distance between the Watson Place and the pilings, maneuvering close to them as she reversed the *Pescadillo*'s engines.

It didn't look like anything exciting. Four metal poles, one at each corner, stuck up out of the water. A wooden platform had been built between the poles, and on top of the platform sat something about the size and shape of a window air-conditioning unit. Beneath the platform was an 18-inch galvanized pipe, the kind used for storm drains to carry rainwater under highways. It extended down into the water.

"If he dropped off drugs here, I don't know where he'd have put them," Frankie said, perplexed. "Like I told you, this thing just measures the water level in the Everglades."

"Let me check it out." Bridger climbed over the side of the *Pescadillo*, stepping onto a wooden support board nailed between two of the posts. Today he'd worn the sandals he borrowed from Steven, but he wore socks, too, and his usual jeans and long-sleeved plaid Western shirt. It was as if he kept all of himself hidden except his face and hands. Jack guessed it was practical, though, since it saved Bridger from sunburn and mosquito bites.

He was so tall he could easily see the top of the platform, but he moved his hands all over it anyway. "Nothing stashed here," he said. "And you can't get down into the galvanized pipe—it's sealed at the top by this box, whatever it is."

"Just the monitor casing," Steven told him.

"Stay there, Bridger," Jack said, "while I take a look at the picture again. Gordon was reaching down...." Jack studied the print carefully. "Look, on your left side, there are two boards nailed together in a V. Feel down at the bottom of the V. Anything there?"

Bridger bent low to touch the place Jack pointed to. "There's a rope," he said. "It goes down in the water."

"Can you pull it up?" Steven asked.

"Yeah. Here it comes."

At the end of the rope hung a tube about four inches wide and two feet long.

"We found it! That must be where the drugs are!" Ashley exclaimed.

Olivia said, "I don't think so. That's just another kind of water monitor. Hand it over into the boat, Bridger."

Bridger climbed back into the *Pescadillo* and gave the tube to Olivia. "These things open up," she said. "Frankie, do you have a toolbox on board?"

"I do. What do you want, a screwdriver?"

"We'll try that for starters," Steven answered.

It took a bit of doing, but they finally opened the tube at the bottom. Another tube slid out of it. It had a faint fishy odor.

"That's it!" Ashley shouted. "I saw one exactly like that lying in the bottom of Gordon's boat when he stopped at the Watson Place."

"You did?" Jack asked. "I didn't notice it." That wasn't too surprising, since Ashley so often picked up on details Jack missed.

Olivia frowned. "This is just the instrumentation for this kind of water monitor. It shows the results of what's being measured—see the numbers here?" She held it up, briefly, then ran the tip of her finger down the column of numbers. "I can read the settings here for temperature, oxygen level, chemicals in the water...."

For a moment, she froze, not breathing, not moving. Slowly, she lifted her eyes to stare at Steven.

"What?" Jack cried.

At the same second, both his parents said, "Chemicals!"

Steven took the tube from her hand. "But all these readings are really low."

"Sure," Ashley said. "'Cause Gordon switched the tubes. Why else would he have one in the boat with him?"

Olivia jumped to her feet. "My manatees! That's why they're sick. He must be dumping some kind of toxic chemical into the water—"

"But no one knows about it because Gordon keeps removing all the readings from the monitors—" Steven broke in.

"—and who knows how long this has been going on?" Olivia finished.

"We gotta find him," Jack declared. "If we prove what he's doing, I'll get my camera back."

"Forget your camera," Frankie scolded. "If what we're thinking here is true, then we need to catch Gordon because he's hurting the Everglades." When her chin jutted out, Frankie's face looked rock hard and stubborn. "Now, these water-measuring devices are placed every ten miles or so—I know where most of them are. If each one has a monitor hanging from it, like the one here, Gordon must go from one to the other changing the tubes. He might be doing that right now. I say we go and try to catch him in the act."

"Wait a minute, Frankie." Olivia held up her hand. "What if we actually find him? He carries a gun. I can't risk my children's safety."

Frankie paused for a moment, then said, "You're right. I'll radio the marine patrol and the park law enforcement rangers. But even if they start out right now, it'll still take them an hour to reach here. Gordon could be long gone by the time the rangers arrive." Agitated, Frankie tapped her chin with her knuckles, considering what to do. "Here's what I think. If we call the marine patrol and the park rangers, and then we go searching for him ourselves, that triples the chance of finding him."

"You know, I want to keep the three kids safe, too," Steven said, "but we could check out the monitors closest to us, and if we do see Gordon, we'll stay far away from him—too far for him to shoot. We'll just let the marine patrol and park law enforcement know exactly where he is. We won't take any chances."

When Olivia hesitated, Jack cried, "Come on, Mom!"

"OK," Olivia agreed. "If that Gordon's the one hurting these manatees, I'd just love to nail him."

"So let's do it," Frankie said. "I haven't been to a good keelhauling in years."

CHAPTER ELEVEN

Frankie's hair whipped off her face in white spikes as she pushed the *Pescadillo* along the calm water. For a while, two dolphins joined them, playfully jumping in the amber-tinted bow waves, but this time the Landons were too distracted to enjoy the sight. Olivia's brow furrowed deeply as she talked of the possibility of toxins in the Everglades waters.

"But why would Gordon dump toxic chemicals around here and then try to cover it up?" Steven asked.

Olivia pushed her sunglasses up the bridge of her nose, where they'd slid down from perspiration. "There're a lot of things I want to find out from that man. What's really bothering me is that if we don't catch him, we may never know the answers. The source of the toxins could be anywhere. It could take years to find it, and meanwhile, more manatees could die—if that's what's causing their sickness."

"It's the Indian curse," Ashley said softly. "Gordon hurts the earth, and it starts to bleed, just like the Indian said."

"It's no curse, it's just foolish humans who don't give a hang about anything but themselves," Frankie declared, her voice tart. As the boat picked up speed, the fresh, salt-tinged air cooled Jack's skin. All but Ashley had crowded forward in the *Pescadillo,* talking and anxiously searching every bend in the Wilderness Waterway, looking for the white boat. Ashley sat in the back, her eyes on the waters behind them. Canoes and a few small fishing boats dotted the passages, along with a couple of boats that had canopies to keep out the sun, but there was no sleek white powerboat to be seen.

"Some of these water-monitoring stations are off the beaten path," Frankie explained as she turned her craft down a narrow passage. "These side routes are a bit tricky, but I think we can navigate this one." Pointing to a fork in the mangroves, she said briskly, "The first device, if I remember right, is beyond that bend. If he's there, we'll pull back behind the trees and radio park law enforcement again to tell them our location." When she cut power, the *Pescadillo*'s speed dropped as they nosed around a clump of trees.

At first, all Jack saw was the sunlight gleaming off the glassy water, so bright it made his eyes ache, and then, suddenly, the sun was hidden by a thick canopy of mangrove branches, and he could see again. At the island's edge, another boxlike water station stood silent and still. There was no person, no boat, no motion, no anything, just leaves from the mangroves hanging limp in the hot, sticky air.

"Nothing here. I didn't really expect any such luck. We'll try the next station," Frankie announced, turning the boat. The channel was so narrow that she barely had room for the maneuver.

After searching out the fifth water station, they stopped to eat lunch on the *Pescadillo*. Frankie had thrown together some sandwiches, filling the cooler with soda pop and fruit. As Jack picked droopy lettuce out of his tuna sandwich, he couldn't help thinking how impossible this plan really was. If Gordon were even just one station ahead of them, the Landons would never be able to see his boat because of all the twists and turns in the Wilderness Waterway; if he were one station behind, he'd be just as much out of sight. There was an even greater chance that the man they were hunting wasn't out in his boat at all, right then. Only Frankie seemed as determined as she had been when they'd first begun.

By the time they reached the ninth station, the sun had moved high in the sky, baking away the morning's fog and leaving a blanket of hot, thick air. Jack was tired. He hadn't slept much the night before. Drowsiness pulled on his eyelids, and the engine's constant drone filled his head until it felt as heavy as an anchor. Stretching, he moved forward and stood next to his parents and Frankie, who was busy poring over a navigational chart of the waterway. "I think I remember one more up there...," she murmured, more to herself than to anyone else.

"Finding him's going to be a long shot, isn't it?" Jack asked.

"Nothing ventured, nothing gained," Frankie replied cheerfully. "We can't find him if we don't look." Her eyes snapped as she added, "If this man's been dumping poison into these waters, then what he's done is nothing short of murder, in my book."

"I understand how you feel, Frankie," Olivia said gently, moving closer to Jack. "I feel the same way, but..."

"...maybe there's no way we can actually find him," Steven finished. "Ten Thousand Islands! The area's just too big."

Frankie stiffened. "A minute ago, I radioed park law enforcement and the marine patrol once again to find out how they're doing. They haven't seen hide nor hair of him." She rubbed the back of her neck, then squinted at Steven, sending a spray of wrinkles down her cheeks. "The thought of him getting away just sits in my craw, but I suppose we're on a wild goose chase."

"How about we look at one more monitoring station," Steven suggested, "and then we'll call it a day. How far to the next one?"

Frankie ran her finger along her chart, the veins on her hand matching the markings on the paper. "We're here, and the next closest station's about three miles down. One more, then." She gave a quick nod and turned the *Pescadillo* west, saying, "This estuary's called Lostmans River. Appropriate, yes?"

Endless mangrove trees huddled at the water's edge, like an army of soldiers stopped in their tracks. Olivia slumped on the bench, fanning herself with Bridger's cowboy hat, and Ashley had her head on her mother's lap. Steven stood next to Frankie, trying to follow their route on the map. Jack's eyes had finally drooped shut, but he heard Bridger, even though Bridger didn't speak all that loudly, when he said, "There he is."

"What?" All of them straightened up fast. Jack was suddenly wide awake.

"Over there. Up ahead."

"Got 'im," Frankie said, slowing the *Pescadillo*. Immediately she radioed park law enforcement, clutching the microphone so tightly her knuckles turned white. "This is the *Pescadillo*," she barked. "We have the suspect in our sight, fellows. We're on Lostmans River, about halfway between Second Bay and First Bay. How soon can you get here? Over."

The radio crackled its answer. "Captain, we're at Alligator Bay. We'll get to you as fast as we can. Maybe a quarter of an hour. How close are you to the suspect? Over."

"Beyond gunshot range, I can promise you that," she answered into the microphone. "And we won't be getting any closer. Over."

"Captain, we're on our way. Hold your position. Over."

Frankie maneuvered the *Pescadillo* into a little notch in the mangrove shoreline. "Jack," she said, "go down into the galley and look on the shelf on the starboard side. There's a pair of binoculars there. Bring 'em up."

Jack hurried down the narrow steps and came back holding the binoculars. "Go ahead, take a look," Frankie told him. "See what he's doing."

He needed a minute to figure out how to focus the binoculars. They looked old and a little worn, but they must have been expensive, because they had wonderful, clear optics.

"Oh my gosh," he exclaimed.

"What?"

"Gordon. He's looking at *us* through binoculars," Jack cried in disbelief. "Now he's putting them down. He going to the console—now he's starting up his boat. There he goes!"

"Looks like he's heading for the Gulf of Mexico!" Steven yelled, then quickly studied the navigational chart. "If he gets out there we'll never catch him."

"We'll never catch him anyway," Frankie muttered, exasperated. "The *Pescadillo*'s about seven times heavier than his open speedboat. He can outrace us something pathetic. I'm radioing park law enforcement again." In her agitation, she had to try several times to rouse someone on the radio. "This is the *Pescadillo*. You guys out there?" she shouted, at the same time steering toward the center of Lostmans River.

"It's not going to work," Bridger exclaimed. "He's pulling way ahead of us. Wow, he's moving fast."

"Stay on him," Steven spoke behind her.

"Wait—where'd he go?" Ashley asked. "I don't see his boat!"

"Behind that bend. Come on...come on...," Frankie urged the *Pescadillo*. When they rounded a crescent-shaped grove of mangroves, Gordon's boat suddenly flashed into view.

"There he is!" Olivia cried. "I see him!"

"Marine patrol, park rangers, come in, somebody! This is the *Pescadillo*. Do you read me? Suspect is heading for the Gulf of Mexico. We are in pursuit. Can you intercept the suspect? Over."

A voice cackled over the line, "Frankie, our craft is not close enough. We'll get there as fast as we can and then try to intercept. Over."

"That Gordon better watch where he's going," Frankie told Steven, squinting at her chart. "At that speed, he can't be minding the depths too well. There are submerged trees around here that got blown down by that hurricane a while back. If he hits one of them—"

She hadn't even finished the sentence before the

white speedboat's hull smacked high out of the water, throwing Gordon loose to arc through blue sky like a rock from a slingshot. Time seemed to hold its breath as his body spun in the air, arms flailing a jangled pattern until he splashed down hard enough to send a fountain of water high against the sky.

The boat landed on its side, righted itself, and kept racing for a tenth of a mile before it turned in a circle. Grabbing the binoculars, Olivia called out, "He's OK. I see one of his arms moving."

"He's got a bigger problem," Frankie called out. "Look at his boat!" The white speedboat, roaring through the water without a pilot, now headed back toward Gordon at full speed, the blades of its motor churning the water into white foam.

"If it hits him, he's dead," Jack yelled.

But the boat turned in a circle, 200 yards away from Gordon. He wasn't splashing or swimming, just hanging in the water, turning himself around to keep watch on his out-of-control boat.

"We can't wait for the park rangers or the marine patrol to get here, so cross your fingers that this'll work," Frankie said, and she shouted, "MAYDAY, MAYDAY, MAYDAY!" into her radio. "This is the motor vessel *Pescadillo* calling the U.S. Coast Guard. Over."

The radio crackled, then Frankie heard, "This is the United States Coast Guard. Captain, what is the nature of your emergency? Over."

"Thank heaven," Frankie breathed, then said, "Coast Guard, we have a boating accident near our location on Lostmans River. We're about three-quarters of a mile upriver from the Gulf. There is one powerboat involved, and it's not mine. And we have a victim in the water and a boat on the loose. Over."

"*Pescadillo,* is the victim wearing a life jacket? Over."

Frankie turned to Olivia. "Can you see if he is, through the binoculars?"

"He's not wearing a life jacket, but he's hanging onto something. It looks like—I think it's a white seat cushion from his boat. It must have flown out of the boat when he hit the tree."

"Coast Guard," Frankie spoke, "the victim is alive and appears to be staying afloat with a safety flotation cushion from his vessel. Over."

For what seemed a long time there was no communication, nothing at all coming over the radio. Olivia kept watching Gordon through the binoculars, and the rest of them focused their rapt attention on the circling speedboat. Then the radio came alive again. "*Pescadillo,* this is the United States Coast Guard. Luckily, we are very close to your location. Hold your position, Captain. We are on our way. Over."

Bridger and Jack cheered, and smacked a high five.

In just a few more minutes, the dull roar of the Coast Guard vessel rose above all other sound. Churning around a knot of mangrove trees, it appeared, tall and gleaming, like an armored knight. "*Pescadillo,* we have the craft and the victim in view," the radio announced. "All is under control. Over."

Over. Jack heaved a big sigh of relief. It really was over. At last.

CHAPTER TWELVE

There's our mama manatee and her baby," Ashley announced, pointing to a drawing on the wall.

"Looks like it," Bridger agreed.

They were in the Everglades National Park Gulf Stream Visitor Center, waiting for Olivia to come out of her meeting, and waiting for Frankie to come and say good-bye.

"Poor Olivia must be exhausted," Steven said. "That meeting's been going on all night."

Jack had been talking to a young woman park ranger named Kelly, who had a warm smile, and bangs that reached her eyebrows. He was telling her all about the man they'd called Gordon. "It turned out his real name is Wallace Lablanc. Want to know how they found out?"

"How?" Kelly asked.

"When the Coast Guard towed his boat out of the water—well, they fished him out first, before the boat—

they had to trace the manufacturer's serial number, and then the place that sold it, because the boat had never been registered. The numbers on the side were fake."

"Really?" Kelly seemed so interested that Jack kept on talking.

"They found out he owns property north of here. Turns out he operates an illegal toxic waste dump."

Kelly had been standing behind the counter at the visitor center, where her job was to answer people's questions about the Everglades—about boat tours, canoe trips, hiking trails, and the birds and mammals whose pictures lined the walls of the center. Making his way slowly, Bridger came over to rest his arms on the counter. Since he was tall, when he leaned forward he was still eye to eye with Kelly.

"Hi," he said. "I'm Bridger. You've got a big map here—maybe you could show me where this guy's toxic waste dump is located. I still can't figure how the chemicals made it down to the Ten Thousand Islands, if he buried the bad stuff farther up north."

"That's a great question," Kelly answered, smiling at him. "It all has to do with the direction the water flows."

Feeling suddenly cut out, Jack frowned as Kelly's attention shifted to Bridger. Anyway, Bridger already knew the answer to that question, so why was he asking it again? Steven had explained that the water table was so high in the Everglades, the toxins leached out, flowed south, and got into the Wilderness Waterway.

"Jack, come here," Ashley called.

Startled, he noticed his sister crouching low on the floor. "Why are you all scrunched down like that?" he asked.

"I want you to take a picture of me with the manatee." A life-size, full-color manatee had been painted on the floor of the visitor center, to let people see the actual length of the animals. "Come on, Jack, please? So I can show all my friends how big a manatee is, compared with me." She wiggled into position in the center of the painting.

"OK. I have to put on the flash attachment first." He'd gladly have taken a dozen pictures of anyone who asked him, because it felt so good to have his camera in his hands again. Once Gordon had been captured, Deputy Carlos had returned Jack's camera with a smile, a pat on the back, and an apology for questioning the kids' story.

After he photographed Ashley on the floor, Jack went all around the visitor center taking pictures of a manatee skull inside a display case, of the egrets, storks, and eagles whose pictures hung on the walls, of the clay Calusa Indian mask under glass....

"Here you all are," Frankie cried, bursting through the doorway. "I need hugs from everyone. I'm going to miss all of you so much."

"We'll miss you too, Frankie," Steven answered, hugging her, "but we've got to get these kids back to school. They've already lost four days."

"Where's Olivia?"

"Still in the meeting."

"That's Frankie," Bridger announced to the ranger named Kelly, shifting even closer to her. "She's the skipper of the *Pescadillo*."

Kelly answered, "Frankie and I have already met, the other day when she brought in the pelican. I'm really sorry about that, Frankie."

All three kids turned toward Frankie. "Sorry about what?" they asked.

She bit her lip and looked down. "I didn't want to tell you. The only thing they could do was cut the fish line off the pelican, take out the fishhook, and release it."

Puzzled, Jack said, "I thought you said it would die without antibiotics."

"Well, it's possible the pelican could survive," Kelly broke in. "If it's lucky. The problem is that the Park Service doesn't have the resources to take care of wounded creatures—unless they're endangered species. We just don't get enough funding or have enough staff. People bring injured wildlife to us all the time, but we can't care for them, so we have to let them go. We feel bad about it, believe me."

"Manatees are endangered," Ashley said.

"That's why we sent out rangers to check on the one you reported. And it's going to be fine," Kelly assured them. "We do what we can. But you know," she added, "if people would just be more careful, and not drop things like fishing lines and plastic bags and rings from six-packs into the water, we wouldn't have so many injured animals."

Just then a door opened and Olivia came out of the back room, followed by three people in Park Service uniforms. Her eyes looked bleary. "Hi, guys," she said. "Karl, Skip, Maureen—this is my gang. My husband, Steven, and my children, Ashley, Jack, and Bridger."

Bridger straightened to stare at Olivia, not sure how to react to her calling him one of her children.

"And there's our dear friend Frankie Gardell," Olivia concluded.

"So what's the verdict?" Steven asked. "Or is there one?"

"Look, I'm beat," Olivia answered. "Let's all go somewhere and get me a cup of coffee, and I'll tell you what we think is happening."

They went to a little restaurant close to the concrete pier beside the visitor center. After all of them were seated, Olivia told them, "Now remember, none of this is definite. It'll take months, maybe even years, before the analysis is complete. But here's what it looks like." She paused while they all ordered a second breakfast—it had been about two hours since their first one. Waffles for everyone except Bridger, who asked for steak and eggs.

"This Lablanc guy," Olivia began, "has made millions storing toxic wastes from computer companies."

"Computer companies!" Jack exclaimed.

"Yes. By-products from printed circuit boards include all kinds of hazardous compounds. The law states that they have to be disposed of properly, but Lablanc wasn't doing that, although he swore to the computer companies that he was. He just dumped the stuff on his property, not caring that it leached into the Everglades. And then he went around to all the water-monitoring stations and changed the chemical readings on the probes, so no one would suspect."

"The jerk," Jack growled. "But Mom, why did it only hurt the manatees, and only some of them? Why didn't it hurt the rest of the wildlife?"

Olivia sipped her coffee and said, "That's why we were up all night, going through dozens of published papers in the Park Service files and on the Internet. As I said, it'll take a lot more study, but we think we have a lead." She paused, then announced, "Copper."

"You mean like pennies?" Ashley asked.

"Right. Copper's an important component in printed circuit boards for computers. And if too much copper gets into the water...." Olivia went on to tell them about a scientific paper published in 1991 that showed a link between copper in river sediments and sickness in manatees. It seemed that in a place called Crystal River, not too far from the Everglades, copper from herbicides had been absorbed by aquatic plants. And manatees ate those plants.

"You know, manatees are big eaters—60 to 100 pounds of vegetation a day, for an adult. So they've probably been absorbing a lot of copper here, too, from the toxic wastes our friend Lablanc—"

"Enemy," Bridger interrupted.

"—dumped on his property. But here's the answer to the real question: Why were only some of the manatees getting sick?"

They waited, all of them focusing on Olivia until Ashley said, "Well, what?"

"Get this—the affected manatees probably spent their winters at Crystal River! Other manatees wintered in other places."

"So?" Jack asked.

"The ones who wintered at Crystal River got a double dose of copper—first from the sedimentary copper that came from herbicides there. And then, when they came back here where Gordon, I mean, Lablanc, was dumping waste from circuit boards, they got even more—the copper that had attached to the plants in the Everglades. That double dose was enough to really hurt them."

"Bravo!" Frankie exclaimed. "You figured it out, Olivia."

"Not all the way. It still has to be proved, and that'll take a long time—we'll compare copper levels in the livers of healthy animals with those in the die-off population. But it's a start, and if it hadn't been for all of you, we wouldn't have a clue."

After they finished eating, they went back to the concrete pier beside the Gulf Stream Visitor Center. At the far end, a big tour boat named *Manatee II* stood moored.

"Let's get some more pictures," Jack said. "Line up, everybody, and look at the camera."

They did—Ashley and Bridger, Frankie, Steven, and Olivia. Then Steven told them, "I have to phone the airline to make sure our flight's on time. I'll be right back."

"OK," Bridger said to Jack, "take a picture of me and the ladies. I want to show it to my dad when I get back to Montana." As Jack peered through the viewfinder, he chuckled a little inside himself at how different Bridger looked. He was wearing Steven's spare sandals on bare feet, a pair of Jack's shorts that were a little too big for Jack, and a T-shirt Steven had bought him with a big manatee printed on the front. But he still had on his cowboy hat.

"Get closer together," Jack instructed, and Bridger, standing between Ashley and Olivia, put his long arms around them both, then stretched to include Frankie in his reach.

"Know what?" Bridger said. "When I came here, I figured if I was lucky I'd get my picture taken with a big trophy fish. But this is better. I'm gonna call this picture 'Bridger Conley with the three smartest, bravest women in the U.S.A.'"

"Why, Bridger," Frankie said with a smile. "That's downright poetic."

"Everybody say cheese," Jack told them. "No! Say mana-TEES!"

"Mana-TEES," they shouted as Jack clicked the shutter.

"Got it!" he said.

AFTERWORD

Solving mysteries is a large part of what wildlife biology is all about: Asking questions, looking for clues, recording observations. These are some of the essential steps in our attempts to peer into the lives of animals and understand how they live.

There has never been a shortage of mysteries in the Everglades. In the past, few white men traveled through the Everglades, partly because of superstitions about and fear of the marsh and its general inaccessibility. Until the middle of the 19th century, the region was described as a "series of vast miasmic swamps, poisonous lagoons, huge dismal marshes without outlet, a rotting, shallow, inland sea, or labyrinths of dark trees hung and looped about with snakes and dripping mosses, malignant with tropical fevers and malarias evil to the white man."

Although the experiences of scientists and visitors

alike have since eased our minds about such fears, the term "mysterious Everglades" still lingers. The mysteries of today range from the whimsical pursuit of the mythical "Skunk Ape"—the South Florida version of Bigfoot—to more serious questions, such as Why has the number of wading birds and other wildlife in the Everglades declined so dramatically? and How can these creatures be restored?

A mystery with similarities to the one you just read about manatees unfolded in early 1989. Biologists working in the Everglades found largemouth bass with mercury levels that were the highest in the state. Mercury, like the copper in this story, is a chemical element called a heavy metal that eventually concentrates in the bodies of the largest predators. Mercury is a nerve poison to people and other animals. Signs were posted at popular fishing spots throughout Everglades National Park warning people about the hazards of eating mercury-contaminated freshwater fish.

In the summer of 1989 one of the few remaining Florida panthers in Everglades National Park was found dead in the Shark River Slough area. A necropsy was performed. It revealed that the animal's liver contained an incredibly high level of mercury—more than a hundred times what is considered safe for people! In spite of this finding, veterinarians were not prepared to list mercury poisoning as the cause of death. They did say, however, that it may have been a contributing factor. Scientists became even more concerned when blood and hair samples taken from living panthers in this area showed higher than expected levels of mercury.

How did these panthers get such high levels of mercury in their systems? Maybe it was in the food they were eating. Scientists examined raccoons, one of the favorite foods of panthers living in Shark River Slough. Tests on raccoons in Shark River Slough showed they had higher levels of mercury than were found in raccoons living in other parts of the park. This was not surprising because these animals feed on mercury-contaminated fish and invertebrates. Since then, mercury has been found in many other predatory species, including spotted sea trout and birds, such as mergansers and cormorants.

Where does mercury come from? How did it get into the environment of Everglades National Park? Scientists have many theories. Mercury does occur naturally as a part of Earth's air, rock, and soil. However, some agricultural and land development practices may release more mercury into the environment. The burning of fossil fuels in power plants and waste incinerators also releases mercury into the atmosphere, often from quite distant parts of the globe. Mercury is found in batteries, dental materials, paints, and other products we use every day. Improper disposal of these products may release that mercury into the environment.

We are still learning what happens to contaminants such as mercury and copper once they enter the environment and what effects they have not only on fish, wildlife, and their habitats but also on human health. It is often years, if not decades, before we are able to prove that a specific chemical is having a harmful effect on our natural resources.

There are other mysteries in the Everglades that are much easier to solve. In fact, they really aren't mysteries at all. For example, I was recently shown a picture of a dead great blue heron. The shriveled and sun-bleached feathers and bones of the bird were hanging from loops of fishing line wrapped around a tree branch along the bank of the Harney River, deep in the Everglades backcountry. Every year countless numbers of water birds, like the pelican in the story, and other marine animals are found entangled in pieces of fishing line and other plastic trash that has been tossed into our nation's waterways by careless people.

Restoring and maintaining a healthy Everglades is an immense responsibility. Ultimately the solution lies with those who care about the future of the Everglades. Those who care about the future of our environment and its living resources—manatees or panthers, pelicans or great blue herons—will remember this: When we throw something away, such as obsolete computers, used mercury batteries, or old fishing line, there really is no such place as "away"—only someplace else! Those who really care will make an effort to reduce, reuse, and recycle.

Skip Snow,
Wildlife Biologist
Everglades National Park

ABOUT THE AUTHORS

An award-winning mystery writer and an award-winning science writer—who are also mother and daughter—are working together on Mysteries in Our National Parks!

Alane (Lanie) Ferguson's first mystery, *Show Me the Evidence,* won the Edgar Award, given by the Mystery Writers of America.

Gloria Skurzynski's *Almost the Real Thing* won the American Institute of Physics Science Writing Award.

Lanie lives in Elizabeth, Colorado. Gloria lives in Salt Lake City, Utah. To work together on a novel, they connect by phone, fax, and e-mail and "often forget which one of us wrote a particular line."

Gloria's e-mail: gloriabooks@qwest.net

Her Web site: http://gloriabooks.com

Lanie's e-mail: aferguson@sprynet.com